A SPORT
AND A PASTIME

A SPORT
AND A PASTIME

JAMES SALTER

THE MODERN LIBRARY

NEW YORK

Library of Congress Cataloging-in-Publication Data
Salter, James.
A sport and a pastime/James Salter.—Modern Library ed.
p.   cm.
ISBN 0-679-60156-2 (acid-free paper)
I. Title.
PS3569.A4622S6   1995
813'.54—dc20   94-45477

Manufactured in the United States of America

2 4 6 8 9 7 5 3 1

JAMES SALTER

James Salter was born in 1925 and grew up in New York City on Manhattan's Upper East Side. From 1938 to 1942 he attended the Horace Mann School in suburban Riverdale. A few early poems, written at this time, were published in *Poetry* magazine. Planning to go to Stanford, at the last minute he instead entered West Point, where his father had gone before him. He graduated in 1945 and began a twelve-year stint in the Air Force, much of it as a fighter pilot.

After flying combat in Korea, he was assigned to air squadrons in Europe and there began writing in his spare time. *The Hunters,* based on war experiences, was published in 1956. The following year Salter resigned his commission to devote himself entirely to writing. A second novel, *The Arm of Flesh,* came out in 1961. "Youthful books," he later said, and though the first, especially, was praised he has refused to have them reprinted.

It was with the appearance in 1967 of *A Sport and a Pastime*—an account of real and imagined passion in working-class France, "Cool, compelling, and brilliantly written," as reviewers noted—that there came a turning point in his career. Though it had limited sales to begin with, it was particularly admired by writers and established his reputation.

In 1975, *Light Years* was published. Dignifying the idea of divorce, it chronicled the gradual dissolution of the twenty-year marriage of a New York City architect and his stunning, unpredictable wife. "This novel—explicitly moody, tender, elegiac," the critic Sven Birkerts wrote, "details the disintegration of a love and the unraveling of a well-knit life. . . . What finally emerges is a novel that is more thrilling than its cadences, its descriptive felicities or evocations of character. It is the sense we get, in places almost overpowering, that its real protagonist is time." Salter's own marriage of long duration broke up the following year.

In the 1960s he wrote a number of films, and in the following decade he began to write stories that appeared in *The Paris Review* and other quarterlies. Increasingly, he shifted his attention to them. Many were published in *Esquire* and afterward included in *O. Henry Prize Stories* and *Best American Stories* as well as anthologies.

Solo Faces, Salter's most recent novel, came out in 1980, the story of rivalry between mountain climbers at the highest level in the Alps. It is also a story of heroism, followed by actions less noble, and of the final struggle to recapture a state of grace.

In 1989, a collection, *Dusk and Other Stories*, won the PEN/Faulkner Award.

For more than twenty years he has divided his time between Colorado, spending winters there for the most part, and Bridgehampton, at the eastern end of Long Island. He lives with the playwright Kay Eldredge. He has two sons and two daughters, another daughter having died in an accident.

Often described as a favorite of other writers and admired for his terse and elegant style, James Salter has gradually become known to a widening number of readers.

INTRODUCTION

"God creates," George Balanchine the choreographer once remarked, "I only assemble." I am reminded by this of my feeling when I began to write *A Sport and a Pastime*—it seemed the book already existed, and it remained for me only somehow to copy it down. Certain parts were easier than others. The beginning took many attempts.

I wrote most of it in a ground floor room on Downing Street in the Village. This was in 1964. The windows gave a view of a drab courtyard and the backs of other buildings, but I had many pages of notes which were, in essence, sketches, and the country I was writing about was not far off—chronologically, that is.

The notes were from 1961–1962 when I had been in France for nearly a year. I had been called back into service during the Berlin Crisis. It was not my first visit to France—I had been smitten long before—but it was the first extended one. I was stationed in the provinces, three hours from Paris, in the area roughly bounded by Nancy, Troyes, Dijon, and Vittel. At its center was the town of Chaumont, my address.

In rearranging the scenery I moved Chaumont south and west to Autun, a somewhat more interesting place although I must admit I have never been able to correctly pronounce the name. I changed the location to be able to state that all characters and events depicted were fictitious. At the same time I think back to a once-infamous book in a locked case in the library which I opened with almost trembling hands and read beneath a similar disclaimer three knowing words someone had penciled in: *without a doubt.*

My ambition was to write a book every page of which could seduce, a book that was flagrant but assured, of imperishable images and obsessions, and above all a book which contrasted the ordinary with—however illicit it might be—the divine. Plainly it is not for me to know the result—it might be the book I intended to write or it might be quite another.

Rereading it after some years I find there are qualities in it I am tempted to admire, and paragraphs that bring memories of where and how they were written, which was often in a kind of fever or trance, as,

> *in that great car that exists for me in dreams, like the Flying Dutchman, like Roland's horn, that ghosts along the empty roads of France, its headlights faded, its elegance a little shabby, in that blue Delage with doors that open backwards, knees touching, deep in the seats, they drive towards home. The villages are fading, the rivers turning dark. She undoes his clothing and brings forth his prick, erect, pale as a heron in the dusk, both of them looking ahead at the road like any couple.*

The question of the novel's narrator is often posed, and how much of what he relates is invented or imagined. Very little, in my opinion. I am impressed by his powers of observation and tend to trust his description of scenes. If he—and he is almost certainly not the author—expresses a degree of disbelief and longing, I can understand it in view of the position in which he has been placed. He has many of my sentiments but the experience is his own.

Submitted to my publishers, Harper Brothers, the book was rejected, described by them as repetitive and uninteresting. There were other rejections. I had begun to lose faith when a friend, William Becker, gave it to the editor of *The Paris Review,* George Plimpton, who instantly accepted it. It was published in 1967 by Doubleday which at the time had an arrangement to do Paris Review Editions.

Poor Doubleday. They had little idea what to make of the book and were uncomfortable with it. A house noted for its large book club and bestsellers, its uneasiness with the profane could be said to date back to 1900 when it published and then immediately withdrew Dreiser's landmark *Sister Carrie* because of qualms about its decency.

Only a few thousand copies of *A Sport and a Pastime* in that edition were sold and a single awkward ad described it as "not a book about baseball." It was, in its way, a hymn—to the small towns and villages, to Paris, architecture, days past, the byways of France, and, of course, to the most incandescent of all earthly pleasures.

It was long ago. I had so few gray hairs I could snip them out with a small scissors. It was winter and cold. I came back from the bar or restaurant late at night and sat alone, darkness surrounding, and wrote. Almost everything I feel and cherish about France came from that year—the vintage for me of the century, one might say.

—JAMES SALTER

"Remember that the life of this world
is but a sport and a pastime . . ."
—*Koran, LVII 19*

A SPORT
AND A PASTIME

September. It seems these luminous days will never end. The city, which was almost empty during August, now is filling up again. It is being replenished. The restaurants are all reopening, the shops. People are coming back from the country, the sea, from trips on roads all jammed with cars. The station is very crowded. There are children, dogs, families with old pieces of luggage bound by straps. I make my way among them. It's like being in a tunnel. Finally I emerge onto the brilliance of the *quai*, beneath a roof of glass panels which seems to magnify the light.

On both sides is a long line of coaches, dark green, the paint blistering with age. I walk along reading the numbers, first and second class. It's pleasant seeing all the plaques with the numbers printed on them. It's like counting money. There's a comfortable feeling of delivering myself into the care of those who run these great, somnolent trains, through the clear glass of which people are staring, as drained, as quiet as invalids. It's difficult to find an empty compartment, there simply are none. My bags are becoming heavy. Halfway down the platform I board, walk along the corridor and finally slide open a door. No one even looks up. I lift my luggage onto the rack and settle into a seat. Silence. It's as if we're waiting to see the doctor. I glance around. There are photographs of tourism on the wall, scenes of Brittany, Provence. Across from me is a girl with birthmarks on her leg, birthmarks the color of grape. My eye keeps falling to them. They're shaped like channel islands.

At last, with a little grunt, we begin to move. There's

3

a groaning of metal, the sharp slam of doors. A pleasant jolting over switches. The sky is pale. A Frenchman is sleeping in the corner seat, blue coat, blue pants. The blues do not match. They're parts of two different suits. His socks are pearl grey.

Soon we are rushing along an alley of departure, the houses of the suburbs flashing by, ordinary streets, apartments, gardens, walls. The secret life of France, into which one cannot penetrate, the life of photograph albums, uncles, names of dogs that have died. And in ten minutes, Paris is gone. The horizon, dense with buildings, vanishes. Already I feel free.

Green, bourgeoise France. We are going at tremendous speed. We cross bridges, the sound short and drumming. The country is opening up. We are on our way to towns where no one goes. There are long, wheat-colored stretches and then green, level land, recumbent and rich. The farms are built of stone. The wisdom of generations knows that land is the only real wealth, a knowledge that need not question itself, need not change. Open country flat as playing fields. Stands of trees.

She has moles on her face, too, and one of her fingers is bandaged. I try to imagine where she works—a *pâtisserie,* I decide. Yes, I can see her standing behind the glass cases of pastry. Yes. That's just it. Her shoes are black, a little dusty. And very pointed. The points are absurd. Cheap rings on both hands. She wears a black pullover, a black skirt. She's a bit heavy. Her brow is furrowed as she reads the love stories in *Echo Mode.* We seem to be going faster.

We are fleeing through the towns. Cesson, a pale station with an old clock. Rivers with barges. We roar through another place, the people on the *quai* standing still as cows. Tunnels, now, which press one's ears. It's as if a huge deck of images is being shuffled. After this will come a trick. Silence, please. The train itself begins to slow a little as if obeying. Across from me the girl has fallen asleep. She has a narrow mouth, cast down at the corners, weighted there by the sourness of knowledge. Her face is turned towards the sun. She stirs. Her hand slips down; the palm comes to rest on her stomach which is already like a Rubens. Now her eyes open without warning. She sees me. She looks away, out the window. Both hands are crossed on her stomach now. Her eyes close once more. We are leaning into curves.

Canals, rich as jade, pass beneath us, canals in which wide barges lie. The water is green with scum. One could almost write on the surface.

Hayfields in long, rectangular patterns. There are hills now, not very high. Poplars. Empty soccer fields. Montereau—a boy on a bicycle waiting near the station. There are churches with weathervanes. Small streams with rowboats moored beneath the trees. She begins looking for a cigarette. I notice that the clasp of her handbag is broken. We are paralleling a road now, going faster than the cars. They hesitate and drift away. The sun is hitting my face. I fall asleep. The beautiful stone of walls and farms is passing unseen. The pattern of fields is passing, some pale as bread, others sea-dark. Now the train slows and begins to move with a measured, a stately clatter as if of carriages. My eyes open. Off in the distance I can see the skeletal grey of a cathedral, the blue outline of Sens. In the station, where for a few minutes we stop, travelers pass along the broken surface of the *quai*, the gravel sounding beneath their feet. It's strangely silent, however. There are whispers and coughs, as if during an intermission. I can hear the tearing of paper on a package of cigarettes. The girl is gone. She has gathered her things and left. Sens is on a curve, and the train is leaning. Travelers stare idly from the open windows.

The hills close in and run beside us as we begin slowly to move away from the city. The windows of houses are open to the warm morning air. Hay is stacked in the shape of boxes, coops, loaves of bread. Above us, the sudden passage of a church. In its walls, cracks wide enough for birds to nest in. I am going to walk these village roads, follow these brilliant streams.

Rose, umber, camel, tan—these are the colors of the towns. There are long, rising pastures with lines of trees. St. Julien du Sault—its hotel seems empty. Shocks of hay now, bundles of it. Great squares of corn. Cezy—the station like scenery in a play that has closed. Pyramids of hay, mansards, barricades. Orchards. Children working in vegetable gardens. JOIGNY is printed in red.

We cross a small river, the Yonne, coming into Laroche. There is a hotel, its roof black with age. Flowers in the window boxes. We stop once more. One changes trains here.

Near baggage carts that seem abandoned we stand around quietly. A cart is selling sandwiches and beer. A pregnant girl walks by and glances towards me as she passes. Sunburnt face. Pale eyes. A serene expression. It seems that people, women especially, have become real again. The elegant creatures of the city, of the grand routes, the resorts, have vanished. I hardly remember them. This is somewhere else. Sheds on the far side of the tracks are filled with bicycles. Workmen in blue sit on sunlit benches, waiting.

From here on the line isn't electrified. The trip is slower. We pass green waters into which trees have fallen. Bitter whiffs of smoke come into the compartment, that marvelous corrosive smoke that eats steel and turns terminals black as coal.

In the corner, in a trenchcoat, her hair gleaming, sits a silent girl with a face like a bird, one of those hard little faces, the bones close beneath it. A passionate face. The face of a girl who might move to the city. She has large eyes, marked in black. A wide mouth, pale as wax. Around her neck is a band of imitation diamonds. It seems I am seeing everything more clearly. The details of a whole world are being opened to me.

The sky is almost completely covered with clouds now. The light has changed, the colors, too. The trees become blue in the distance. The fields turn dry. There are tunnels of hay, mosques, cupolas, domes. Every house has its vegetable garden. The roads here are empty—a motorcyclist, a truck, nothing more. People are traveling elsewhere. Outside a house two small cages are hung for the canaries to get some air. We are passing bricks of hay, casques. We are laboring along. The acid smell of smoke comes and goes. The long, shrill blasts of the whistle, lost in the distance, fill me with joy.

She has taken a caramel out of her handbag. She unwraps it, puts it in her mouth to ensure her silence. Her fingers play with the paper, rolling it slowly, tightening the roll. Her eyes are pale blue. They can stare right through one. The nose is long but feminine. I am curious to see her teeth.

She touches her hair, first beneath one ear, then the other. Her wedding ring seems to be enameled. An umbrella with a violet canopy is strapped to her luggage. The handle is gold, no thicker than a pencil. No polish on her fingernails. She sits motionless now and stares out the window, her mouth curved in a vague expression of resignation. The little girl who is opposite me cannot take her eyes from her.

I begin to look out the window. We are coming close now. Finally, in the distance, against the streaked sky, a town appears. A single, great spire, stark as a monument: Autun. I take my bags down. I have a sudden, little spell of nervousness as I carry them along the corridor. The whole idea of coming here seems visionary.

Only two or three people get off. It's not yet noon. There's a single clock with black hands that jump every half-minute. As I walk along, the train begins to move. Somehow it frightens me to have it go. The last car passes. It reveals empty tracks, another *quai,* not a soul on it. Yes, I can see it already: on certain mornings, on certain winter mornings this is almost completely hidden in mist; details, objects come forth slowly as one walks. In the afternoons, the sun imprints it all with cold, bodiless light. I pass into the main room of the station. There's a newsstand with iron shutters. It's closed. A large scale. Schedules on the wall. The man behind the glass of the ticket window doesn't look up as I walk by.

The Wheatlands' house is in the old part of town, built right on the Roman wall. First there is a long avenue of trees and then the huge square. A street of shops. After these, nothing, houses, a Utrillo-like silence. At last the Place du Terreau. There's a fountain, a trifoil fountain from which pigeons are drinking, and looming above, like a great, beached ship: the cathedral. It's only possible to glimpse the spire, studded along the seams, that marvelous spire which points at the same time to the earth's center and also the outer void. The road leads around behind. Here many windows are broken. The lead frames, formed like diamonds, are empty and black. A hundred feet farther is a small, blind street, an *impasse,* as they say, and there it stands.

It's a large, stone house, the roof sinking, the sills worn. A huge house, the windows tall as trees, exactly as I remember it from a few days of visiting when, on the way up from the station I had a strange conviction I was in a town I already knew. The streets were familiar to me. By the time we reached the gate I had already formed an idea that floated through my mind the rest of the summer, the idea of returning. And now I am here, before the gate. As I look at it, I suddenly see, for the first time, letters concealed in the iron foliage, an inscription: VAINCRE OU MOURIR. The VAINCRE is missing its C.

Autun, still as a churchyard. Tile roofs, dark with moss. The amphitheatre. The great, central square: the Champ de Mars. Now, in the blue of autumn, it reappears, this old town, provincial autumn that touches the bone. The summer has ended. The garden withers. The mornings become chill. I am thirty, I am thirty-four—the years turn dry as leaves.

2

This blue, indolent town. Its cats. Its pale sky. The empty sky of morning, drained and pure. Its deep, cloven streets. Its narrow courts, the faint, rotten odor within, orange peels lying in the corners. The uneven curbstones, their edges worn away. A town of doctors, all with large houses. Cousson, Proby, Gilot. Even the streets are named for them. Passageways through the Roman wall. The Porte de Breuil, its iron railings sunk into the stone like climbers' spikes. The women come up the steep grade out of breath, their lungs creaking. A town still rich with bicycles. In the mornings they flow softly past. In the streets there's the smell of bread.

I am awake before dawn, 0545, the bells striking three times, far off and then a moment later very near. The most devout moments of my life have been spent in bed at night listening to those bells. They flood over me, drawing me out of myself. I know where I am suddenly: part of this town and happy. I lean out of the window and am washed by the cool air, air it seems no one has yet breathed. Three boys on motorbikes going by, almost holding hands. And then the pure, melancholy, first blue of morning begins. The air one can bathe in. The electric shriek of a train. Heels on the sidewalk. The first birds. I cannot sleep.

I stand in line in the shops, no one notices. The girls are moving back and forth behind the counters, girls with white faces, with ankles white as soap, worn shoes going at the outside toe, dresses showing beneath the white smocks. Their fingernails are short. In the winter their cheeks will be splotched with red.

"Monsieur?"

They wait for me to speak, and of course it all vanishes then. They know I'm a foreigner. It makes me a little uneasy. I'd like to be able to talk without the slightest trace of accent—I have the ear for it, I'm told. I'd like, impossible, to understand everything that's said on the radio, the words of the songs. I would like to pass unseen. The little bell hung inside the door rings as I go out, that's all.

I come back to the house, open the gate, close it again behind me. The click is a pleasing sound. The gravel, small as peas, moves beneath my feet and from it a faint dust rises, the perfume of the town. I breathe it in. I'm beginning to know it, and the neighborhoods as well. A geography of favored streets is forming itself for me while I sleep. This intricate town is unfolding, detail by detail, piece by piece. I walk along the river on the bank between two bridges. I stroll through the cemetery that glitters like jewelry in the last, slanting light. It seems I am seeing an estate, passing among properties that will someday be mine.

These are notes to photographs of Autun. It would be better to say they began as notes but became something else, a description of what I conceive to be events. They were meant for me alone, but I no longer hide them. Those times are past.

None of this is true. I've said Autun, but it could easily have been Auxerre. I'm sure you'll come to realize that. I am only putting down details which entered me, fragments that were able to part my flesh. It's a story of things that never existed although even the faintest doubt of that, the smallest possibility, plunges everything into darkness. I only want whoever reads this to be as resigned as I am. There's enough passion in the world already. Everything trembles with it. Not that I believe it shouldn't exist, no, no, but this is only a thin, reflecting sliver which somehow keeps catching the light.

Cristina Wheatland—she was Cristina Cabaniss and born Cristina Poore—has a cool face, a little bony, and large, pale eyes. Her father was an ambassador. They led a brilliant life. She went to school everywhere, Argentina, Greece, the Philippines. I don't remember just how Billy met her, only that she was twenty-three and they fell in love right from the start. She was just getting her divorce. He was the one she should have married in the first place. He knew how to handle her. He's the only man who knows how to make her feel like a woman.

"Isn't that right, sweetheart?" she says.

"That's right, Bummy."

He's selecting cubes of ice from a silver bucket and talking with his back turned. She sits at the far end of the room, her legs curled beneath her. Paris. It's three in the morning. Their daughter, the servants, the whole building is asleep. She leans forward to let me light her cigarette and then falls back, floats really, into the soft cushions. She can't live in America any more, she says. That's the only thing that bothers her. She's gone back to visit. It just isn't for her. In the first place, she doesn't even know how to drive. Billy hands her the drink. She gives it back.

"Sweetheart," she says, "I only wanted a half."

He walks to the end of the long room once more. I see him pick up a new glass. There's a mysterious slowness to all his movements, it's almost as if he is thinking them out. Even so, they have the grace of a dream. Billy Wheatland—he was on the hockey team, a great forward, one of the best ever as they always say, and forever surrounded by friends. You never saw him alone. He was standing in front of a mirror, combing black hair still damp from the shower. When he smiled, a little, heroic scar gleamed in his lip.

He comes back with the second drink and hands it to her without a word.

"I adore you," she says.

He sits down and crosses his legs. He's wearing expensive shoes. Cristina is running her fingers inside the strand of single pearls around her neck, back and forth. To me, Billy says,

"Well, you know it's very quiet down there. I mean it's a very small town. You were there, but I don't think you realize."

They begin to talk about whom he can write a letter to for me. I sit there listening and feeling a mild excitement, like a child in front of whom a year at boarding school is being discussed.

"The water's turned off," he says. "I don't even know how to turn it on. There's an agent who handles all that. We've never been there during the winter."

But a letter will handle that, too, or he can call. It's arranged. I'm going down, any time I like. Cristina begins talking to him. I hardly hear. A glory of which I could not speak filled me then like a shimmering of sunlight. It was the ten thousand famous photographs Atget had made of a Paris now gone, those great, voiceless images bathed in the brown of gold chloride—I was thinking of them and of their author, out before dawn every morning, slowly stealing a city from those who inhabited it, a tree here, a store front, an immortal fountain.

I saw before me the calm, the sheltering of many diligent hours while this town of mine exposed itself to me, its only stranger, day by day. Of course, the whole thing was impulsive. I didn't mention it to a soul, these ideas can vanish. I went no further than imagining the moment I displayed them all for the first time. Morning in the gallery. The prints are being turned over, one by one. Ashes fall softly to the table. A hand distractedly brushes them away. Do you like them? I stand there still fresh with the aura of Europe. Even my clothes were bought there. I wait for the answer. These can make you famous, he says finally. I am dizzied. For a moment I permit myself to believe it.

"How big is it actually?"

Billy doesn't know. He turns to her.

"It's very small," Cristina says.

"Fifteen thousand," he guesses.

"It's not that small," I say. "It's bigger than that."

"It's small," he warns. "Believe me."

Beloved town. I see it in all weathers, the sunlight falling into its alleys like fragments of china, the silent evenings, the viaduct blue with rain. And coming back— this is much later—there are long, clear stretches with fields on either side, and we fly down an aisle of trees, the trunks all white with lime. Roads of France. Restaurants and cemeteries. Black trees and hanging rain. The needle is on one-forty. The axles are cracking like wood.

The Grand Hotel Saint-Louis. The small court with its tables and metal chairs. Shutters of inside rooms pushed open through a wall of dense ivy. Grillwork is buried within it, forgotten balconies. Above, a section of the sky of Autun, cold, clouded. It's late afternoon—the green is trembling, the smallest tendrils dip and sway. That penetrating cold of France is here, that cold which touches everything, which arrives too soon. Inside, beneath the *coupole,* I can see the tables being set for dinner. The lights are already on in the marvelous, glass consoles within which the wealth of this ancient town is displayed: watches in leather cases, soup tureens, foulards. My eye moves. Perfumes. Books of medieval sculpture. Necklaces. Underwear. The glass has thin strips of brass like a boat's running the edges and is curved on top—a dome of stained fragments, hexagons, hives of color. Behind all this, in white jackets, the waiters glide.

Small, mirthless town with its cafés and vast square. New apartments rising on the outskirts. Streets I never knew. There are two cinemas, the Rex and the Vox. Water is falling in the fountains. Old women are walking their dogs. Morning. I am reading *An Illustrated History of France.* There's a dense mist which has turned the garden white, in which everything is concealed. An absolute quiet. I hardly notice the passing of time. When I go out, the sun is just burning through. The spire seems black. The pigeons are grumbling. There's always the desire to talk to somebody about this time, I can't escape it. I start out beneath the long, sulking flank of the cathedral and then begin descending. I know all the streets. Place d'Hallencourt. Rue St. Pancrace, curving down like a woman. I know the fine houses. And, of course, I know some people. The Jobs—she's the thinnest woman I think I've ever seen. The waitress at the Café Foy. Madame Picquet. Now, that—I have to ask Wheatland about her.

3

The elevator rises, hushed, to a splendid apartment above the Avenue Foch. The rooms are filled with people, some of them in evening clothes. The Beneduces have given a small dinner. Everyone else was invited to come by afterwards. Two waiters in white jackets are serving coffee. I stand near the window. Below, through the dark and still fragrant trees, the traffic floats past on headlights. Paris seems wondrous to me now, even a little too rich. I'm strangely devout, I find myself defending the meager life of the provinces as if it were something special. It's not like the life of Paris, I say, which is exactly like being on some great ocean liner. It's in the little towns that one discovers a country, in the kind of knowledge that comes from small days and nights.

"There's Anna Soren," Billy whispers.

She has been a famous actress, I recognize her. The debris of a great star. Narrow lips. The face of a dedicated drinker. She constantly piles up her hair with her hands and then lets it fall. She laughs, but there is no sound. It's all in silence—she is made out of yesterdays. He is pointing out Evan Smith, whose wife is a Whitney. There are girls who work in the fashion houses, publishing. One meets a certain kind of people here, people with money and taste.

"Definitely."

"There's Bernard Pajot."

Pajot is a writer, short, the face of a cherub with moustaches, enormously fat. His life is celebrated. It begins in the evenings—he sleeps all day. He lives on potatoes and caviar, and a great deal of vodka. He not only looks like, they say he *is* Balzac.

"Does he write like him?"

15

"It's enough of a job looking like him," Beneduce confides.

I overhear Bernard Pajot. His voice is deep and richly hoarse. He smokes a thin, black cigar.

"Last night I had dinner with Tolstoi . . ." he says.

Behind him are tiers of fine books laid on glass shelves and illuminated from below like an historic façade.

". . . we were talking about things that no longer exist."

Beneduce is a journalist, a bureau chief. Straight, brown hair which he wears a little too long, blue eyes, unerring knowledge. He has the calm irreverence one achieves only from close observation of the great. And he knows everybody. The room is filled with marvelous languages. People from Switzerland. People from Mexico. His wife is a lynx. Even from across the room she imposes her assurance, her slow smiles. She's a friend of Cristina's, I know her from afternoons on the boulevard. I see her leaving cafés. She favors knit suits, her breasts moving softly within them, but I don't think she meets men. Her husband is too potent. He could cut them to pieces. He'd know exactly how to do it.

She's talking to Billy. He's very elegant, very slim. Hair, I notice, turning grey along the sides. Everything else has become gold, the chaste gold of cufflinks, a gold watchband, the mesh dense as grain, a gold lighter from Cartier. I don't know what they're talking about, nothing, I'm sure it's nothing because I've had a thousand conversations with him myself, but still he can hold her there somehow, Billy, to whom Cristina used to whisper in those early days that she wanted to leave the party and go make a little boom-boom. He has that white line of a scar on his mouth. One's eyes always fall to it. He lights her cigarette. Her head is bent forward a little. Now it straightens up. They continue to talk. I notice she's never really still. She seems to writhe in one's gaze with slight, almost imperceptible movements.

I wander away towards more quiet regions of the apartment which is very large. The ceilings become silent, the voices fade. It seems I am entering an older, a more conventional household. The dining room is empty and dark. The table is just as it was, not cleared. The cloth is still spread on it, the chairs are in disarray. Glass plates bear the remnants of brie and the halves of pears already becoming brown. In front of the windows is a zone of tall plants, a conservatory through which noise does not penetrate, through which, in the daytime, the light diffracts. It is a room in which I can imagine the silence of leisurely mornings, the pages of *Le Figaro* turning softly as Maria Beneduce glances over them, the pages of the *Herald Tribune*. She is in a short robe printed with flowers. She drinks black coffee stirred with a tiny spoon. Her face is natural and unpainted. Her legs are bare. She is like a performer backstage. One loves this ordinary moment, this pause between the brilliant acts of her life.

Suddenly someone is behind me.

"Did I scare you?" Cristina says, smiling.

"What? No."

"You jumped about a foot," she says. "Come on, I want you to meet somebody."

A friend from Bristol, Tennessee, she tells me as she leads me back. No, but I'm going to like her, she's very funny. She's married to a rich, rich Frenchman. She puts flowers in all the bidets. He gets furious. Already I dread her.

People are still coming in, even this late, appearing after other dinners, the theatre. Beneduce is guiding a handsome trio into the room, a man and two stunning

women in suede boots and tightly belted coats. Mother
and daughter, Cristina tells me. He's marrying them
both, she says. Near the bar Anna Soren listens to the conversation around her with a wavering, a translucent
smile. She doesn't always know who's speaking. She
looks at the wrong person. Her false eyelashes are coming
loose.

"You know something?" Cristina says. "You're the
only friend of Billy's I like."

It pleases but disturbs me, this remark. I'm not sure
what it means, I just have the feeling it will prove to be
fatal. I don't want to answer or even to appear as if I've
heard.

"They're all illiterates," she tells me.

Through the crowd a woman is approaching.

"Isabel!" Cristina cries. It's her friend.

There is no way to begin except with admiration for
Isabel who is forty and dressed in a beautiful, black Cha-
nel suit with silver buttons and a ruffled, white shirt. On
her finger is a ring with a large diamond, a perfectly
round diamond that catches every piece of light, and her
smile is as dazzling as her clothes. There's a young man
with her whom she introduces.

"Phillip . . ." Her hand flutters hopelessly, she's forgotten his name.

". . . Dean," he murmurs.

"I'm the worst in the world," she says, the words
drawling out. "I just seem to forget names as fast as people can tell them to me."

She laughs, a high, country laugh.

"Now, don't take it to heart," she tells him. "You're
the best-looking thing in this room, but I'd forget the
name of the President himself if I didn't already know it."

She laughs and laughs. Phillip Dean says nothing. I
envy that silence which somehow doesn't disgrace him,

which is curiously beautiful, like a loyalty we do not share.

"He's been traveling in Spain," she says, "isn't that right?"

"Spain!" Cristina says.

His face seems to show it. There still remain the faint, lustrous tones of journeys in an open car.

"I love Spain," Cristina says.

"You've been there?"

"Oh," she says, "many times."

"Barcelona?"

"I love it."

"And Madrid . . ."

"What a city."

"We went to the Prado every day," he says.

"I love the Prado."

"What is it?" Isabel says.

"The museum."

"The museum?" she says. "Why, I love it, too. I forgot what it was called."

"It's the Prado," he says.

"Why, that's right. I remember it now."

"What were you doing in Spain?" Cristina asks.

"I was just traveling," he says.

"All alone?"

Images of a young man in the dun-colored cities of late afternoon. Valencia. Trees line the great avenues. Seville at night, the smell of dust that has settled, the smell of oleander, richer, green. In front of the big hotel two porters are hosing the sidewalk.

"No, I was with my father," he says.

Suddenly I like him. Cristina can't take her eyes away. She asks when he was born, and it turns out he's a Sagittarius which is a very good sign.

"Really?"

"It's one of the best for me," she says. "Scorpio is the worst."

"I'm a Libra," Isabel says and laughs. "Isn't that right?"

Dean has a small, straight mouth and wide-set, intelligent eyes. Hair that the summer has dried. It's of schoolboy heroes that I am thinking, boys from the east, ringleaders, soccer backs slender as girls.

"You have a great face," Cristina says. She is seized with a sudden gaiety. "You know, I'd like to do a painting of you."

Isabel laughs. The evening has only begun.

At three in the morning—Cristina never goes to bed when she's drinking—we are wandering through the disorder of les Halles. The air is chilly at this hour, noises seem to ring in it. The workmen glance up from their crates at the unmistakable sound of high heels. Isabel is talking. Cristina. They are pointing everything out. We trail foolishly between great barricades of fruit and produce, past empty bars, through the carts and trucks. Finally we emerge at the roaring, iron galleries where meat is handled. It's like coming upon a factory in the darkness. The overhead lights are blazing. The smell of carnage is everywhere, the very metal reeks with an odor denser than flowers. On the sidewalk there are wheelbarrows of slaughtered heads. It's right out of Franju and that famous work which literally steams of it. We stare down at the dumb victims. There are scores of them. The mouths are pink, the nostrils still moist. Worn knives with the edge of a razor have flensed them while their eyes were still fluttering, the huge, eloquent eyes of young calves. The bloody arms of the workers sketch quickly. Wherever they move, the skin magically parts, the warm insides pour out. Everything is swiftly divided. An animal which two minutes ago was led to them has

now disappeared. Cristina draws her white coat around
her like a countess.

"I'm going to have nightmares," she says.

"We're really going to sleep sometime?" Billy asks.

"Let's go to the pig place," Isabel says.

"Sweetheart, where is it? Isn't it right around here?"

"It's just down the street," Billy says.

It takes us ten minutes to find it. Of course, there's an
enormous crowd, there always is this time of night. Taxis
are waiting with their lights on dim. Cars are parked everywhere. The restaurant is filled. There are tourists,
wedding parties, people who've been to cabarets, others
who've stayed up in order to visit the famous market. It's
said they are planning to move it to a location outside the
city, it will soon be gone.

Somehow we find a table. Billy is rubbing his
hands. There's a delicious odor of rich, encrusted soup
which is the specialty. Cristina doesn't want any, she
wants wine.

"It's not good for you, you know that," Billy tells her.
She's had jaundice, she was in bed for months. "Why
don't you just have some soup?"

"You have it," she says.

"Bummy . . ."

"What?"

"I'm going to order it for you."

"Go right ahead," she says. She turns and gives us a
brilliant smile.

The crowd is thick. The waiters struggle to get
through. They seem to hear nothing, or it has no effect.
The patrons are multiplying as if in a dream. Incredible
faces on every side, Algerian, bony as feet, cardboard
American, the pink of French. Isabel is laughing, laughing. She claps her hand over her mouth and rocks back
and forth a little. She's telling about an argument that

started when her husband was packing for a trip. He was shouting at her in French.

"Now, you obey me this instant," he said.

"I will not." She performed some angry, little stamps.

"Stop doing that with your feet."

"I won't." Laugh, laugh.

Of course, he adores her, I know they're going to tell me that.

"Don't ever marry a Frenchman," she says. Then she laughs. She is hugging Coco, her poodle, and laughing. She is opening boxes from Lanvin, the tissue crashing as she brushes it aside. The telephone rings, and it's one of her friends. She laughs and laughs, she talks for hours.

"Do you live in Paris?" Dean asks me.

"Pardon?"

"Do you live in Paris?" he says.

Isabel is telling about her husband's family. She's sick of them. All they're interested in is their grandbaby, she says. I explain I'm living in the Wheatlands' house. It's in a little town.

"You know Dijon?"

"Yes."

"It's near Dijon."

"It's in the center of France," he decides.

"The very heart. It's a small town, but it has a certain quality. I mean, it's not rich, it's not splendid. It's just old and well-formed."

"What town is it?"

"I doubt if you've ever heard of it. Autun."

"Autun," he says. Then, "It sounds like the real France."

"It is the real France."

"He's crazy," Billy warns.

It's almost five in the morning when we drive Isabel home. There are just the four of us left, Dean has gone. I am exhausted. I feel as if I am entering a grave crisis of the soul. The streets are completely abandoned. The sky has begun to pale. We pull up before a building on the Avenue Montaigne, Billy takes her to the door. I stay in the car with Cristina, our heads leaning back, our eyes closed.

"He's a nice boy," she says. "Don't you wish you were that young again?"

"I'm not that old."

"Baby . . ." she says soothingly.

"I only feel it."

"No, you look very young. Really. You look as if you could still be in school."

"Thank you."

"What were you like then?" she says sleepily.

"It's too long ago."

"No, really, what were you like?"

"I was the idol of my generation."

I can hear her head move.

"Didn't you know that?" I tell her.

The door opens, it's Billy. He slumps down in the seat. We start to drive.

"Let's go somewhere for a drink," Cristina says.

He is silent.

"Billy?"

"Do you really want to?"

"Where can we go?"

"The Calvados," he says.

"Yes," she says, "let's go there."

C ourtyards with rusty gates receive me back. Enclo-
sures. Great walls crumbling at the sill. The trees
stand like brewers in the Place d'Hallencourt.
Bricks are laid beneath them. The sidewalks are veined
with moss. As one descends, the streets begin to flower
out. Rue Dufraigne. Faubourg St. Blaise, a fine house
here, small iron balcony, enormous garden. The trees
pour over the wall and shade the public side as well. The
doors look quite secure.

There's another house on rue de la Grille. A marvelous color—faded brick, with the doors, windows, all the
major lines set in white stone. Gravel driveway. Tall, iron
gates. I pass it in the morning as a girl in a pink smock
opens the shutters room by room. Belongs to a doctor, I'm
sure. They're all doctors. *Vétérinaires. Yeux, nez, gorge,
oreilles.* They're fortified within the most solid houses in
town, the biggest ones, commanding every street. The fix-
tures are polished. The plaques are always shined.

Posters for football stuck in the windows of cheap
cafés. Autun against Charolles. Autun against Chagny.
No one seems to read them. A few men are playing dominoes; they look like North Africans. At the bottom of
town the factories are silent. The old ones have been
abandoned, tanneries with their tall chimneys cold, their
windows dark. Beyond, the river lies still.

Four in the afternoon. The trees along the street, the
upper branches, are catching the last, full light. The stadium is quiet, some bicycles leaning against the outer
wall. I read the schedule once again and then go in, turning down towards the stands which are almost empty.
Far away, the players are streaming across the soft grass.
There seem to be no cries, no shouting, only the faint thud
of kicks.

24

It is the emptiness which pleases me, the blue dimensions of this life. Beyond the game, as far as one can see, are the fields, the trees of the countryside. Above us, provincial sky, a little cloudy. Once in a while the sun breaks out, vague as a smile. I sit alone. There are the glances of some young boys, nothing more. There's no scoreboard. The game drifts back and forth. It seems to take a long, long time. Someone sends a little boy to the far side to chase the ball when it goes out of bounds. I watch him slowly circle the field. He passes behind the goal. He trots a while, then he walks. He seems lost in the journey. Finally he is over there, small and isolated on the sideline. After a while I can see him kicking at stones.

I am at the center of emptiness. Every act seems purer for it, easier to define. The sounds separate themselves. The details all appear. I stop at the Café St. Louis. It's like an old schoolroom. The varnish is worn from the curve of the chairs. The finish is gone from the floor. It's one large, yellowing room, huge mirrors on the wall, the same size and position as windows, generous, imperfect. Glass doors along the street. Wherever one looks, it seems possible to see out. They're playing billiards. I listen without watching. The soft click of the balls is like a concert. The players stand around, talking in hoarse voices. The rich odor of their cigarettes . . . They're never there in the daytime. It's very different with the morning light upon it, this café. Stale. The billiard table seems less dark. The wood is drawing apart at the corners. It's quite old, at least a hundred years I should think, judging from the elaborate legs. Beneath the pale green cloth which is always thrown over it, the felt is worn, like the sleeves of an old suit.

"*Monsieur?*"

It's the old woman who runs the place. False teeth, white as buttons. Belonged to her husband probably. I can hear them clattering in her mouth.

"Monsieur?" she insists.

Later on, about nine, there's the hotel where there's music in the bar and somebody at least, a few couples, sitting around. The three or four gilded youths of the town, too, slouched on the divans. I know them by sight. One is an angel, at least for betrayal. Beautiful face. Soft, dark hair. A mouth like spoiled fruit. Nothing amuses them—they don't talk until somebody leaves, and then they begin little, laughing cuts, sometimes calling over to the barman. The rest of the time they sit in boredom, polishing the gestures of contempt. The angel is taller than the rest. He has an expensive suit and a tie knotted loosely at the neck. Sometimes a sweater. Soft cuffs. I've seen him on the street. He's about seventeen, and he seems less dangerous in the daylight, merely a bad student or a boy already notorious for his vices. He's ready to start seductions. Perhaps he even says it's easy, and that women are simple to get. To believe is to make real, they say. A chill passes through me. I recognize in him a clear strain of assurance which has nothing to imitate, which springs forth intact. It feeds on its own reflection. He looks carefully at himself in the mirror, combing his hair. He inspects his teeth. The maid has let him undress her. She hates him, but she cannot make him go. I try to think of what he's said. He has an instinct for it. He is here to hunt them down, to discover the weaklings. I don't know what he feels—the assassin's joy.

I am modeling myself after him, just for the evening. As I walk home I see my image floating on the glass of darkened shopfronts. I stop and look at clothes. It's like coming out of a movie. I have discarded my identity. I am still at large, free of my old self until the first encounters, and now I imagine, very clearly, meeting Claude Picquet. For a moment I have the sure premonition I am about to, that I am really going to see her at the next corner and, made confident by the cognacs, begin quite naturally to talk. We walk along together. I watch her closely as she speaks. I can tell she is interested in me, I am circling her like a shark. Suddenly I realize: it will be her. Yes, I'm sure of it. I'm going to meet her. Of course, I'm a little drunk, a little reckless, and in an amiable condition that lets me see myself destined as her lover, cutting into her life with perfect ease. I've noticed you passing in the street many times, I tell her. Yes? She pretends that surprises her. Do you know the Wheatlands, I ask. The Wheatlands? Monsieur and Madame Wheatland, I say. Ah, *oui*. Well, I tell her, I'm staying in their house. What comes next? I don't know—it will be easy once I am actually talking to her. I want her to come and see it, of course. I want to hear the door close behind her. She stands over by the window. She's not afraid to turn her back to me, to let me move close. I am going to just touch her lightly on the arm . . . Claude . . . She looks at me and smiles.

Mornings with clouds. Windy mornings. Mornings with black wind rushing like water. The trees quiver, the windows are creaking like a ship. It's going to rain. After a while the first silent drops appear on the glass. Slowly they increase, cover it, begin to run. All of Autun beneath the cool, morning rain, the sculptures on the Roman gates streaking and then turning dark, the slate roofs gleaming now, the cemetery, the bridges across the Arroux. Every once in a while the wind returns, the rain moves sideways, beats against the windows like sand. Rain falling everywhere, on all the avenues and enterprises, the ancient glories of the town. Rain on the plate glass of the Librairie Lucotte, rain on les Arcades, on au Cygne de Montjeu. A long, even rain that makes me quite content.

5

He arrives in the late afternoon. It's the first week of October and the weather has been mild—pulled up before the gate in a splendid old car which yields nothing to popular taste is Phillip Dean. Of course, it's a complete surprise, perhaps I show it.

"Listen, I hope I'm not disturbing you," he says, almost shyly.

"No, not at all."

"I just thought I'd drive down."

"Well, I'm glad you did." After a moment I add, rather foolishly, "Is this your car?"

Yes, he insists I admire it, a convertible standing low and journey-dark in the dusk. We walk around to the front. There's an enameled nameplate with letters of blue: Delage.

"Oh, this is a famous make. I thought they'd gone out of business."

"They have," he says. "This is a 1952."

We circle it slowly.

"I fell in love with it right away," he says.

It *is* a marvelous looking machine. Dean trails behind me, pointing out details. The headlights are like washbasins.

"I've only had it four days."

It belongs to a friend of his who isn't able to drive it enough. Dean is just using it.

"Do you want to take a ride?" he asks. "Come on. You have to get in the other side."

Cool, October evening. The seats are chilled and smell of leather. The doors shut with a heavy, unequivocal sound. He inserts the key and starts it up. All the needles leap.

"It's a dream to drive," he says. "It goes like the wind."

"I can imagine."

"No, really, it does."

"How fast?"

"I don't know yet," he says. "I'm creeping up on it."

We drive along the curving, mysterious streets. The shutters are already closed throughout town. People are coming home from work, some on bicycles, most of them walking. I can see the pale of their faces as they turn to look at the car. It has Paris plates. They have no idea whose it is, of course.

We cross the square and go down the long, open street that runs to the station, bicycles swimming beside us, their faint headlights quivering on the road. The line of dark trees continues the entire length and then, turning, leads to the open space in front of the station, the hotels across the way, the bus terminal to one side with its lighted booth that takes four photos for a franc. There are two taxis waiting. The drivers—one is a fat woman with glasses—are in the hotel bar, wrapped in the congenial odor of tobacco and wine. They have nothing to do until the train arrives.

We stop for a moment and look back up towards town. Sitting in the car makes it all very privileged. The air is melancholy and dark. People walk by bent on their errands. Behind us the river flows.

It's getting cold in the car. As we drive back, I ask if there's any heat.

"It doesn't work," he says, "but I think I can fix it."

We park at the Foy and he lifts the hood.

"Look at that," he announces.

It's a distillery of ducts and hoses.

"I used to work on motorcycles," he says. "Of course, this . . ."

". . . is a little more challenging."

"We must think of it as three motorcycles," he says. "Everything becomes simple."

He touches the hoses, searching for the one which leads to the heater.

"Can you find it?"

"Oh, eventually," he says, rising up.

We go into the café. There are booths on each side and a row of tables in the middle. A small bar. A small dance floor. Towards the back they're playing cards. The place is almost empty, though. They all come later and sit in white silence before the television. We take a booth near the front. Dean's already decided to stay over. I told him there was the whole house.

"I'm going to drive all around tomorrow," he says. "I'd like to explore the countryside."

Through the doorway I can see people looking at the Delage.

"Your car's creating a sensation."

"In Paris," he says, "they figured I was at least a duke. At the hotels, you know, the doormen would open the door. Salute. *Bonjour, monsieur.* I'd give them a little nod."

"You didn't speak."

"A few words of Spanish," he says modestly. "Can you eat here?"

"Are you hungry?"

"A little. I can wait."

"We'll have dinner at the hotel."

After a pause, he says,

"Uh, I don't have much money with me . . ."

"Don't worry."

"I'm supposed to get a check," he says. "I should have had it two days ago."

"Don't worry about it," I reassure him.

"Do you know many people in town?" he asks.

"Oh, a few," I say. "It's pretty quiet."

"Quiet," he says. The idea seems to settle in. "Well, I mean, how quiet?"

"It's quiet," I tell him. "Shall we have one more?"

We arrive at the hotel about eight. The dining room is well lit, it seems even brighter than usual. Perhaps it's my mood. After all, it is an event, I've been eating alone. We open the menus. Our heads lower a bit to consider things. Around us are the soft, reassuring sounds of dining. In the center of the room a table gleams with fruit. Beside it is a tray of cheeses: bleu de Bresse, heavy and rich, pungent as a woman's armpits; roquefort, veined like marble; the small, wrapped chévres; gruyère . . . And now I notice for the first time, near the entrance, a party that includes Mme. Picquet and her little girl. They're all talking agreeably. I don't know who the others are. They're much older. They could be relatives. Anyway, I've found out a little about her. She's been divorced. Her husband fell in love with another woman. Claude was too abundant for him, perhaps, too sumptuous. She's always carefully made up, her hair arranged and laid across her brow. Bracelets on each wrist. Big rings, one of them on her left index finger. She even wears it when she types. She might be twenty-eight, Claude, or twenty-nine. When she walks, she leaves me weak. A hobbled, feminine step. Full hips. Small waist. Her legs are a little thin. I see her in the Hôtel de Ville, where she works. She leans over the typewriter, erasing. There's a glint of white slip where her sweater parts slightly at the bosom. My eyes keep going there in quick, helpless glances.

Her divorce was very expensive, she told me. I noticed the mole painted on her cheekbone. It cost four hundred dollars, she said, and her husband four hundred, too, and besides that, she had to give him almost all the furniture, this vanished husband who was an eyeglasses salesman and had to travel a lot. She makes a little gesture of resignation.

Her daughter sits beside her, attentive, composed. She's eight years old and already as marvelously slow of movement as her mother. Quite a pretty child. She eats with a fork that is too big for her. She glances up at Claude from time to time.

Dean has a healthy appetite, but after the second glass of wine there's a tendency for things to fall from his fork. He casually eats them right from the tablecloth. We're having *quenelles* made from river pike, *quenelles de brochet*. He keeps asking me what they're called.

His French is better already. Of course, the waiter pretends not to understand him. Dean doesn't care.

"They're all like that," he says. "*Quenelles*. Is that right? What did you tell me?"

Long, unhurried hours of evening, the car parked outside where light from the entrance falls on it, people pausing to look, the winter coming on. Plates being silently removed, the taste of foods lingering. The immortal procession of a French meal. We've finished the wine. Dean is pouring Perrier water into his glass. He's thirsty as a horse, he says.

"They always tell you drink wine to be safe."

"Yes, but I drink the water."

"Everywhere, so do I," he says. "You know where the cleanest water in the world is?"

"No."

"The Yale swimming pool," he says. His voice is fading. "Anyway, that's what they always told us."

"When did you get out of Yale?"

"I didn't," he says. "I quit."

"Oh."

He describes it casually, without stooping to explain,

but the authority of the act overwhelms me. If I had been an underclassman he would have become my hero, the rebel who, if I had only had the courage, I might have also become. Instead I did everything properly. I had good marks. I took care of my books. My clothes were right. Now, looking at him, I am convinced of all I missed. I am envious. Somehow his life seems more truthful than mine, stronger, even able to draw mine to it like the pull of a dark star.

He quit. It was too easy for him, his sister told me, and so he refused it. He had always been extraordinary in math. He had a scholarship. He knew he was exceptional. Once he took the anthropology final when he hadn't taken the course. He wrote that at the top of the page. His paper was so brilliant the professor fell in love with him. Dean was disappointed, of course. It only proved how ridiculous everything was. He'd already been given a leave in his freshman year, now he took another. He went to see a psychiatrist. He lived with various friends in New York and began to develop a style. It lasted a whole year, but the university was very understanding. Finally he went back and did another year, but in the end he quit altogether. Then he began educating himself.

6

D ean at the washbasin, shaving. Standing there half-naked, he seems very thin. He has bony shoulders. I am trying to create details. Narrow, white feet. I am trying to make him real, the darling of his father's friends. He visited their houses. He drove their cars.

The bathroom is enormous with a window crossed

by low shelves bearing Cristina's bottles, many of them
filled with color, bath salts, toilet water, apothecary jars.
The razor scrapes like a barber's, short, even strokes and
then a pause. He cleans it with occasional bursts of water.
His beard isn't heavy. It's mostly around his chin. In the
outer room, fully dressed, I sit waiting. He inspects himself hastily in the mirror.

"You ready?" he asks innocently.

Those first, early weeks with the cold skies of Europe
covering them, weeks that seem now never to have been,
that later events washed out of existence, almost out of
memory. In October we went—I am taking these from a
list—to Châlons-sur-Seine, to Beaune, Dijon (three times),
and even to Nancy.

Over the crown of western hills we sail beneath a brilliant sky of clouds shot through with sunlight and begin
the descent to town, the road cutting back and forth in
deep, blind turns. And then those great, lineal runs
through neighborhoods I knew nothing of, making
straight for the perfect square which marked the city like
a signet. Nancy. How could I know? Streets that later
would become as sacred to me as those of my childhood.
Boulevard Georges Clemenceau. We pass it and are gone.

It's Saturday. The streets are crowded. Men are roast-
ing chestnuts on the corners. We sit near the window of
the Café du Commerce. Four in the afternoon. The blue
sky of France flooding with clouds. The last of the year
upon us, the cold coming on—one can feel it every day.
Dean is studying the guidebook. I stare out the window.
Around the square cars turn, slow as oxen. Occasionally a
Jaguar or Mercedes goes past, one of those great, ghost-
ing machines and sometimes a lovely face inside. The
shops are jammed with shoes, gold ornaments, suedes,
beautiful cheeses.

I see it at dawn now, when the light is chalky and

then the palest blue. The streets are absolutely still. The huge *portes* are silent—Place Carnot, its long regiment of trees. I wander this city like a somnambulist. The blue cigarette smoke is rising, the odor of reminiscences, in the Bar de la Division de Fer. Avenue du XXme Corps. The veterans sit hunched in their sweaters, their blue suit-coats, surrounded by the relics of a glory now spent, gone to rust, the white hand of mould staining it, the smell of dampness. Dawn comes in the flat windows of the cafés. They walk home alone, along the canal, their shoes scuffing the grey sidewalk.

Autumn nights. We stroll in the early darkness, deciding where to eat, and start for home in the first flurries of snow, bundled up and breathing vapor in the old Delage. The heater is still no good. Snow is streaming into the headlights, pouring against us, exploding on the glass. The gear box is grinding away. Taking a curve, we begin to snake wildly.

"Oh, watch it, Dean," he says.

Across the road a river of snow is flowing, spilling sideways, shifting, rushing away. We begin to drive slower. The snow beats white against us, making no sound. We are lost in a whirling whiteness, in the rich voice of the car.

"Did you see that sign? What did it say?"

"Langres, I think."

"Langres," he says.

"Yes. We're on the right road."

It takes hours. After a while, there's no other traffic. We're sailing along roads as deserted as the steppes. The villages are dark.

When we finally arrive, we stop in at the Foy. It's nice to enter, to be inside. The wood of the floor feels good. We sit down in one of the booths. There are some couples scattered around. It's all very cosy. The waitress brings us tea. She's a girl from the country who works here on weekends, I've seen her before. She wears a turtleneck sweater, black skirt, a leather belt cinched tightly around her waist dividing her into two erotic zones. Behind the bar the radio is going softly. Outside, the snow is falling, covering the car like the statue of a hero, filling the tracks that lead to where it is parked. Dean watches as she removes the things from her tray and sets them on the table: cups, saucers, the silver pot. His eyes follow her as she walks away.

"She likes you," I tell him.

His gaze jumps to me, hesitates.

"What do you mean?"

"Well, I can tell," I say.

He looks at me and then glances at her. She's leaning against the bar, paying no attention. Dean smiles then, tired and lonely.

"That's right," I tell him.

"I know. She's been dreaming about me for weeks," he says.

7

Madame Job, passionately thin, bony as a boy, thinks he looks like an actor: Eddie Constantine. When I tell Dean this, he says,

"Who?"

I explain that it's somebody who appears in cheap films.

"I've never heard of him," he says.

"You'll see him. I don't think you look like him, but anyway . . ."

"It's wild," he says.

Madame Job is smiling. She doesn't speak any English. She follows the conversation from mouth to mouth, like a dog.

The room has a bare, modern look. Somehow inexpensive, too. Rugs are scattered over a floor of polished wood. There are a few magazines on a table. The furniture almost seems to be there on loan. I don't know if there's a reason. Henri Job works at the glove factory. He's a manager, quite important. Billy wrote a letter to him for me. When I called, they were very friendly. Of course, this isn't his house, it belongs to her father. It's just next door to her father's house in fact—not an unusual situation.

Henri doesn't come from here. He's from Lyon. Ah, that second greatest city of France, beside its wide river. He holds this over her like a title. Her father has done very well in *chauffage*—he has the biggest shop in town—but, after all, Lyon. One can see it all in her face. Besides that, he's quite strict. He doesn't permit her to dance, a thing she loves madly she confided to me. It's he who has the bad heart, but nevertheless ...

A bitter, foggy week in November. We drove along the Boulevard Mazagran without seeing another pair of headlights. The lime trees were black as iron in the dark. We turned off on the street where the Jobs live in a newer section of town. Blank walls. Everything looks abandoned, even the cars parked along the curb. I've already warned Dean that the evening will probably be boring. Many of the houses along here are recent. It's like a new planting, they simply haven't become anything yet. There are embarrassing spaces between them, bare trees.

The Jobs have a wire gate, a green gate which I close behind me. The sound of our feet seems very loud in the neighborhood silence.

"Are you sure this is the night?" Dean says. No lights are visible.

We walk on flat stones set in the gravel, past a concrete fishpond that has only a few dead weeds in it. I ring. A light comes on overhead, and Madame Job appears. She greets us warmly. I introduce Dean there, in the narrow hallway, with an inconvenient shaking of hands, and we walk in to the sitting room, Madame Job behind us, turning off lights.

After dinner there are slides of Austria, taken on their last trip. Henri holds them up like coins before he projects them. Distant views of mountains. Hotels that are slightly askew. Madame Job took that one, he explains in English. She hears her name. She smiles.

"It's one of her best," Henri says.

Dean sits silently in the darkness. It was quite a good dinner—roast chicken, endive, *mousse au chocolat*. Her desserts are marvelous. I have the feeling she is glancing at him unseen.

"Innsbruck," Henri says.

I look back at the screen. A vast, ocher city materializes in a sequence of fragments like hints of a great image which has been shattered. We are confronted with the brilliant parts. Corners of streets. Trollies. Splendid fronts of buildings too far distant to really see. I sit there receiving occasional draughts of Madame Job's perfume. I'm surprised at its strength. There's not much flesh for it to draw warmth from—those skinny arms. She has marvelous skin, though. Her face seems very clean.

"Ahh," she breathes, admiring one of the slides. She says to me.

"*Ça c'est joli, n'est-ce pas?*"

"*Formidable*," I say.

Dean sits there like a superior child. He says nothing. Of course, it's the monotony of the whole evening that he finds incredible, that there really can be a couple like this. (Henri is forty, perhaps. Juliette about twenty-nine. But Dean has read Radiguet. Twenty-nine isn't old.) His silence, his self-removal seem almost visible. He lights a cigarette. In that closed room with its central shaft of light, the smoke leaves his mouth with a dense brilliance. He breathes a long plume of it, bluer than ice. Henri holds another slide up to the light. We are moving east now. It seems they stopped every ten kilometers to take pictures of something.

Dean would never go on a trip this way, I'm certain. I'm a little jealous of what he might do, I feel he's just coasting at the moment. I imagine him on a journey to the south of France in the spring. I'm not certain who's with him. I know he isn't alone. They are traveling cheaply, with that touch of indolence and occasional luxury that comes only from having real resources. They live in Levi's and sunlight. Sometimes they brush their teeth in streams. Perhaps she's the young whore he met in Paris he found so easy to get along with. No, that's a banal idea. I've had it myself: teaching her how to dress, wear her hair, behave, speak, and all the while abusing her like a convict morning and night, some of the instruction being offered whilst in union, so to speak. Yes, she finds it amusing. She takes off her clothes with a smile. They have a relationship like the beginning of *Manon Lescaut*. They wander through the cities. They vanish into hotel rooms—one cannot follow. There are long silences filled with things I ache to know . . .

Afterwards, sitting in the car, the leather icy, the windows opaque from the fine, endless rain, he wants to drive somewhere.

"Where?"

"Let's go to Dijon," he says.

"Are you serious?"

"It's not that far."

I feel a little guilty, as if somehow they can sense our joy at being outside at last. It's after eleven, but he's completely awake. He devours my weariness.

"Come on," he says.

We make our way slowly back to the main street, the wipers moving in discord, groaning as they cross the glass. It's an absolutely dark, abandoned town at this hour, only a few cafés still open. As for the rest of it, every building is black.

"He's really nasty to her," Dean says.

"What do you mean?"

"He's got her right there in his hand," he says, "and he's just, you know, breaking her bones."

"I don't think it's that bad."

"I feel sorry for her," he says.

"Why? She's all right. She made a good marriage. They have children, her husband's doing well. It's all important. I mean, you have to understand things. They have their own pleasures."

"She's starved," Dean says.

"A little, probably. It's because you were there tonight."

"Maybe." He smiles.

"Listen, when someone thinks you look like a movie actor, that's something right there."

"Yes."

"Especially when you don't even resemble him."

Dean laughs.

Dijon is hung in mist. We drive along empty streets. He knows the way perfectly. In front of us the blue neon of the Rotonde appears. We park and walk to the door. Now we can hear music, out of place in the fog, the silence. When we step inside, the darkness shatters like glass. On a little stage rimmed with light a band is playing. Couples are dancing, everything is very loud.

The waiter wants us to order champagne. Dean shakes his head: no, no. He knows the routine. We sit there watching it all.

"What music," he says.

"Do you think it's good?"

"Christ, no," he says.

In the middle of the crowd is a girl with an African—I'm certain he's a student—in a cheap grey suit. They have their arms around each other. As they dance it's like a playing card revolving. The jack of spades vanishes slowly, the queen of diamonds is revealed. Their mouths come together in the dark.

Across from us there are more Negroes, but these are Americans. Soldiers. One can see it immediately in their faces, their clothes. They have thick mouths, a certain crudity. And they're big. They have great hands, broad shoulders. They seem ready to burst out of their clothes. There are Coke bottles on the table—for their French girls, of course. One of them sits in a skimpy, plaid dress, green I make it to be. Short-sleeved, though the night is cold. She turns her head a little. She's very young. Pure, expressionless features. Suddenly I am in anguish, I don't know why—she obviously cares nothing—but somehow because of her predicament. She looks sixteen. Her young arms flash softly in the gloom.

Now one of them begins talking to her in that rich, melodious under-language. She doesn't understand him—perhaps it's the noise of the band. He leans closer. His mouth is moving just next to her ear. She nods her head then. She looks at him calmly and nods. The others are sitting with their huge forearms on the table, listening to the music, occasionally passing a word. I can't see the other girl very well. Her hair is quite long. The music is crashing around us. The drummer's face is wet.

We have traveled from Innsbruck to bedlam. It's no longer possible to talk. I'm very sleepy and suddenly a little depressed. I keep looking across to their table. When they leave, I am sure I know exactly how it will be. They'll go out to a big, green Pontiac at least five years old, maybe a Ford. The muffler is broken. The sound of the engine is powerful and raw. She sits between two of them in the back. That means . . . I don't really know what it means, what low, graceful phrases are offered in the dark. As Rilke says, there are no classes for beginners in life, the most difficult thing is always asked of one right away. Still, they are not so bad, these black men. They are very sweet, I have heard, they are very tender. They will spend every penny they have on a girl, absolutely every- thing. They are foolishly generous. I envy them for that.

We drive in silence through a dense fog which swal- lows the headlights of the car. The yellow beams are smoking before us. Nothing can be seen. La Rotonde is very distant. The doors have closed behind us, the music has disappeared. We crawl down invisible roads, barely faster than a walk. The drive home will take hours, the last hours of a night which we have left behind. We've given it to the soldiers. They possess nothing. They with- hold nothing. When the bill comes they reach in their pockets vaguely and ask each other for coins.

I have the window partly open. The damp air leaks on my face.

"I have to learn more French," Dean says.

"Well, that'll come. I see you writing down words all the time."

"The trouble is it's all food," he says. "That's the only thing I can talk about. You can't just keep talking about food."

"You're right. You should read the newspapers."

"I'm going to start."

We are sneaking past the outskirts of Dijon, only oc- casionally passing anything we recognize, an intersec- tion, a particular sign.

"I'll tell you what's great about this country," he says suddenly. "The air. Everything smells good.

"It's the real France," he says. "You were right. I'd never have discovered it if it weren't for you."

"Oh, you would have."

"No, I'd just be hanging around Paris like everybody else. It's easy to do that. But who goes to Dijon?"

"Not too many people."

"Or Autun?" he says.

"Fewer."

"Nobody," he says. "That's what makes it."

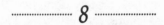

T he mornings are growing colder, I enter them unprepared. Icy mornings. The streets are still dark. The bicycles go past me, their parts creaking, the riders miserable as beggars.

I have a coffee in the Café St. Louis. It's as quiet as a doctor's office. The tables have chairs still upturned on them. Beyond the thin curtains, a splitting cold. Perhaps it will snow. I glance at the sky. Heavy as wet rags. France is herself only in the winter, her naked self, without manners. In the fine weather, all the world can love her. Still, it's depressing. One feels like a fugitive from half a dozen lives.

These dismal mornings. I stand near the radiator, trying to warm my hands over iron that's cold as glass. The French have a nice feeling for simplicity. They merely wear sweaters indoors and sometimes hats as well. They believe in light, yes, but only as the heavens provide it. Most of their rooms are dark as the poorhouse. There's an odor of tobacco, sweat and perfume, all combined. A dispirited atmosphere in which every sound seems cruel and isolated—the closing of a door, footsteps beneath which one can detect the thin complaint of grit, hoarse *bonjours*. One feels part of a vast servitude, anonymous and unending, all of it vanishing unexpectedly with the passing image of Madame Picquet behind the glass of her office, that faintly vulgar, thrilling profile. As I think of it, there's an ache in my chest. I cannot control these dreams in which she seems to lie in my future like a whole season of extravagant meals if only I knew how to arrange it. I see her almost daily. I can always go down there on some pretext, but it's difficult to talk while she's working. Oh, Claude, Claude, my hands are tingling. They want to touch you. In her elaborately done hair there is a band which she keeps feeling for nervously. Then she touches the top button of her sweater as if it were a jewel. Around her neck there are festoons of glass beads the color of nightclub kisses. A green stone on her index finger. And she wears several wedding bands, three, it seems. I'm too nervous to count.

"You're not from here, are you?" I had asked her.

"Oh, no. I am from Paris."

"I thought so."

She smiles.

"But do you like it here?" I said.

"Oh," she shrugs helplessly.

When I am near her I can almost experience the feel of her flesh, taste it, like a starving man, like a sailor smelling vegetation far out of sight of shore.

She opened her purse and took out photographs of herself made in the salons of hotels. It happened too quickly, I wanted to look at them longer. She had been a mannequin, she said. She traveled around to do shows in those days. It was very nice. Weekends in Vichy, she told me . . . weekends in Megève.

December the third. A day that promises nothing, that passes quickly. In the afternoon, a light snow, a snow so faint and small-bodied that it seems nothing more than a manifestation of the cold. The town is already in that rapid descent towards darkness, the lighted shops appearing, headlights, restaurants, the small cafés. Everything else is turning black in a great, incorruptible cycle, too serious, too ancient to vary, while behind the shutters and heavy curtains an evening life is measured out in mean portions, as exact as those of an old shopkeeper.

I stop for a paper in the bookstore. I know the old man there very well. The counter is near the window where the light catches him flat on, like a cabinet minister before breakfast. He's wearing a heavy sweater and a scarf. His cheeks are absolutely purple. He seems very mournful, but there is all the winter still to be survived. He no longer lives in years; he is down to seasons. Finally it will become single nights, each one perilous as a lunar journey. He hands me the change. His fingers are rough as wood.

In a room with every light burning, Dean opens wide his arms.

"Where've you been?" he says. "I have a surprise for you."

"What?"

He doesn't answer right away.

"You're going to be pleased," he assures me, stopping before the mirror to look at himself from one angle, then the other, his movements light as a bird's. *Mon vieux*, he is singing to himself off key, *vous êtes beau, vous êtes beau.*

"Well, aren't you going to tell me?" I ask him.

"Oh, in time," he says, "in time."

I watch him tie his shoes. He's finished dressing. Now he inspects himself full-length.

"It's snowing," I say.

"Snowing!" He goes straight to the window. He can see it. "Ahh!"

"That pleases you?"

"Perfect," he says. "It's just perfect."

We go off to the Foy.

Certain things I remember exactly as they were. They are merely discolored a bit by time, like coins in the pocket of a forgotten suit. Most of the details, though, have long since been transformed or rearranged to bring others of them forward. Some, in fact, are obviously counterfeit; they are no less important. One alters the past to form the future. But there is a real significance to the pattern which finally appears, which resists all further change. In fact, there is the danger that if I continue to try, the whole concert of events will begin to fall apart in my hands like old newspaper, I can't bear to think of that. The myriad past, it enters us and disappears. Except that within it, somewhere, like diamonds, exist the fragments that refuse to be consumed. Sifting through, if one dares, and collecting them, one discovers the true design.

The Etoile d'Or. One lighted room along a cold street, the snow descending fitfully, the traffic thin. The waiter is a young boy in a soiled, white jacket. Only one other table occupied—by a man reading the newspaper—in this modest room, this room of a country house, almost empty in the flat of winter, the dark, icy hours. The three of us over the printed cloth, she quite nervous. It shows in her hands. Her ears are pierced, I notice. Through the tender flesh of the lobes cheap ornaments are hooked, and she touches them from time to time. She looks exactly as she looked in Dijon that night. The same dress. The same white arms. The waiter comes with three trays of oysters, deep, irregular shells within which the bodies lie, pure and glistening. For a moment she sits motionless as we begin to eat and only then begins herself, as if in respect or an unwillingness to appear hungry. The real reason is much simpler: she was watching us, she'd never eaten oysters before.

Anne-Marie Costallat, born October 8, 1944. I was beginning high school and masturbating twice a day, curling over it like a dead leaf, when she was born, in a bed of violets, as she says—all French mothers tell their children that. Dean tries to offer her some wine. *Non,* she says, *merci.* It isn't good for her. Her cheeks are a little red from the cold, but the closer one gets the more marvelous-looking she is. Eighteen, I think! She seems even younger. It frightens me, of course. Eighteen, and a nigger for a lover. Right out of Jean Genet.

"How did you meet her!" I say. I realize my voice is strained. She's excused herself. The W.C. is in the next room, past the bar.

"What do you think of her?" he says.

"She's only a child."

She ate like a dockhand, leaning over the plate and taking big forkfuls. She finished all the bread.

"Did you notice that?"

Of course. I remembered it forever.

"Food," he says.

"Yes?"

"My big subject."

She is returning. She sits down with a little smile.

By ten, the waiter has vanished. The restaurant is silent, and the chill of cheap hotels begins to surround us. She is speaking English, but it's hard to understand and very funny. She smiles when we laugh, a tentative, friendly smile.

"Comment?" she asks.

She worked six months for the U. S. Army in Orléans. That's where her English is from, although she's forgotten a lot. Then she worked in a hotel in Troyes. (I've never seen this place. I can only imagine it—a small, commercial hotel, quite modern. Roland is the son of the owner. He and his friends all have cars. They have parties, and there's a big, empty house that belongs to one of them where they can take the girls . . .) This summer she will get a job in La Baule. Where is that, Dean wants to know. Brittany, I tell him. It's on the coast. She nods. I'm not sure she understands much of what we're saying. Dean puts his jacket over her shoulders. It's become very chilly in the room.

We drive her home. Place du Carrouge. The building she lives in is dark. Her room is over an alley where some Corsicans have a fruit business. The tissues from lemons, pears, the oranges of Spain, blow fitfully along the pavement. They have an old truck, lofty and battered, which is always parked close to the store. It's a section of town I have somehow never seen, one of those quiet backwaters of a few houses and streets that don't run very far. I sit in the car while Dean takes her to the door, but first she comes to the window on my side. I hurriedly roll it down.

"Bon soir," she says politely.

He leaves her at the door, and up to her room she goes like any good child, a room on the top floor, probably, under the roof, like a sparrow. This room—a squad of inspectors could never find it—in a narrow building. This room I am never to visit. From the first, when I asked him about it, he said nothing. There wasn't much to describe, it was a room. The meagerness of that reply told it all.

He was afraid of what I might ask him. He was almost ready to lie—it's easy enough to tell. I used to lie constantly. Now I've stopped. With Dean, I never spoke anything but the truth, right from the beginning. Partly, I suppose, I was afraid he might find me out, but more important, lies suddenly seemed useless. It was even more than that, they gave me no comfort. I felt, with him—it's difficult to explain—that he could not be challenged by lies. He had already proved he cared nothing for them. That was the whole point of his life.

She stoops with the match, inserts it, and the heater softly explodes. A blue flame rushes across the jets, then burns with a steady sound. There's no other light in the room but this, which reflects from the floor. She stands up again. She drops the burnt match on the table and begins to arrange clothing on the grill of the heater, pajamas, spreading them out so they can be warmed. Dean helps her a bit. The silk, if it's that, is quite cold. And there, back from the Vox opposite the Citroen garage, its glass doors now closed, they stand in the roaring dark. In a fond, almost brotherly gesture, he puts his arms around her. They hardly know one another. She accepts it without a word, without a movement, and they wait in a pure silence, the faint sweetness of gas in the air. After a while she turns the pajamas over. Her back is towards him. In a single move she pulls off her sweater and then, reaching behind herself in that elbow-awkward way, unfastens her brassière. Slowly he turns her around.

She leaves his kisses finally to stand against the wall, arms at her sides.

"Jeanne d'Arc," she says. The tremulous blue plays across her. Her features seem resigned.

He takes her by the arms. She turns her face to the light. He is her executioner, she says. The word thrills him. His knees tremble.

He puts her to bed in her warm pajamas. She is innocent, he decides. She smiles softly, the calm of a long convalescence in her face. Finally he turns to go, but at the door her voice stops him. Yes? Turn out the light, she says. He does. Like Lucifer, he creates darkness and he descends.

I see myself as an *agent provocateur* or as a double agent, first on one side—that of truth—and then on the other, but between these, in the reversals, the sudden defections, one can easily forget allegiance entirely and feel only the deep, the profound joy of being beyond all codes, of being completely independent, criminal is the word. Like any agent, of course, I cannot divulge my sources. I can merely say that some things I saw myself, some I discovered, for after all, the mutilation, the delay of as little as a single word can reveal the existence of something worthy to be hidden, and I became obsessed with discovery, like the great detectives. I read every scrap of paper. I noted every detail.

Some things, as I say, I saw, some discovered, and some dreamed, and I can no longer differentiate between them. But my dreams are as important as anything I acquired by stealth. More important, because they are the intuitive in its purest state. Without them, facts are no more than a kind of debris, unstrung, like beads. The dreams are as true and manifest as the iron fences of France flashing black in the rain. More true, perhaps. They are the skeleton of all reality.

I am the pursuer. The essence of that is I am the one who knows while Dean does not, but still it is far from even. To begin with, no matter what I do, I can never uncover everything. That alone is enough to make him triumph. I can never anticipate; it is he who moves first. I am only the servant of life. He is an inhabitant. And above all, I cannot confront him, I cannot even imagine such a thing. The reason is simple: I am afraid of him, of all men who are successful in love. That is the source of his power.

She was waiting for him at six. It was already dark, and they drove through the thrilling streets, past shops that were open late, their windows alight. She goes up to get her things, including her little radio, and they drive to St. Léger, a small factory town, her town. Her house is by the canal. There they park and Dean waits for her in the car. A fine rain is falling. Men are still walking home from work, whistling, along the dark street. He cannot see them. Their voices arrive unexpectedly, like those in a church. He sits quietly. He listens to them cough, go by, and then gets out to walk along the bank of the canal. Bicycles pass. Some girls or women, he cannot tell, stop to look at the car. They are trying to see inside—he can make out the tableau by streetlight—their bicycles held upright in one hand, the metal of the hood glistening with points of rain. The rest of it, the long elegant line, is lost to shadow. Suddenly they turn towards the house where the door has just opened. Fluorescent light spills out and the murmur of voices. He hurries to meet her at the car.

She's told her mother everything, she announces as they drive off.

"Everything?" he says.

"*Oui.*"

They drive for a while in silence, coming to the main road.

"Eh, what did she say, your mother?" he asks.

"*Est-il prudent.*"

"What?"

She shrugs. She doesn't know how to explain it.

"*Prudent,*" she repeats.

In Troyes they stop at her old hotel to ask if she has any mail. He can see her through the glass doors. They hand something to her, a single letter which, as she comes out, she puts in her handbag without reading.

They have dinner in the Brasserie Lorraine. An old

dachshund, his paws turned white, sits by the bar. Sometimes he wanders among the tables or goes to the door
and barks to go out. A waiter opens it for him. When he
comes in again, he lies down with moans. Hesitations. At
the end, a sigh. One can hear him breathing.

In every respect a wonderful dinner. She is talkative
and happy. The food seems spread around her like vege-
tables to a roast. She is simply the living portion of the
meal, and she smiles at his appetite which embraces her
with glances.

Outside, in the small *place*, cars are parked in a center
triangle. The night is hung with the thinnest of rains.
They sit in silence, waiting for the check. Finally it arrives,
the last obstacle is removed. From here it is straight-
away, a long flight down the road to Paris, headlights cast
ahead, the engine thrumming. Dean drives in cool excitement, in the electric hush of tires. He has a hard-on half
the time and wonders if there will be any trouble register-
ing in the hotel. If it had been me—and sometimes I am so
drenched with images that I think it was—but if it had
been, I would have had no confidence, none at all. I
would have been exhausted, wrung by disbelief, going
ahead only out of a sort of curiosity, to discover exactly
where it would all vanish. I would have thought: God
will not permit it.

The rain passes. There are scattered clouds with the
moon behind them. The sky is brighter than the land.
Annie is sleeping, curled up in the leather seat. He wakes
her as they enter Paris. They drive along the river through
light traffic and then down Rue de Rivoli, her favorite.
She watches the passage of the long, immaculate arcades
like a tourist. Then she takes out a mirror to inspect her
face.

There is no difficulty. A porter takes them upstairs
and along the corridors, the carpet creaking beneath their
feet. He has the key in his hand. They come to the door.

He inserts it. They wait behind him. The lock rattles. At last the room is revealed. It is classical and large. The objects within it, their arrangement, the colors all seem as if they have been together a long time, assembled by use. There is nothing recent or frivolous. A huge bed at which Dean quickly glances. Windows admitting streetlight. Mirrors. Chairs. A large bathroom in which the heat seems on.

He goes down to park the car. Finding a place is difficult. He cruises along the narrow streets. He doesn't want to just leave it in a driveway. When he comes back, she is combing her hair. Except for a pair of the cheap, black panties one finds on the counters in Monoprix, she is naked. She smiles at him, a little stiffly, a little uncertain.

The water is running. In the bathroom he turns her around admiringly. She is very complaisant with all her clothes off. She moves readily to his touch. She's quite beautiful. Slim. A bit of dark hair between her legs. They stand beneath the shower. He nestles himself flat in the meeting of her buttocks. An excruciating *douche.* He feels unable to move, but he begins to soap her breasts which glisten like seals beneath the flow of water. He scrubs her back. Between the shoulder blades the skin is broken out in small, red points. He goes over them with the cloth. It's good for them, he tells her. Aureate light is reflected from the ceiling. He has a hard-on he is sure will never disappear.

He has wrapped her in an enormous towel, soft as a robe, and carried her to the bed. They lie across it diagonally, and he begins to draw the towel apart with care, to remove it as if it were a bandage. Her flesh appears, still smelling a little of soap. His hands float onto her. The sum of small acts begins to unite them, the pure calculus of love. He feels himself enter. Her last breath—it is almost a sigh—leaves her. Her white throat appears.

When it is over she falls asleep without a word. Dean

lies beside her. The real France, he is thinking. The real
France. He is lost in it, in the smell of the very sheets. The
next morning they do it again. Grey light, it's very early.
Her breath is bad.

I cannot follow them through the city that day,
through the December streets, avenues as bitter as the
steppes. They have only a little money, I know that. They
shop all afternoon and buy nothing. Then, tired of walking, they return to the hotel. Dean has to go on an er-
rand—he needs a part for the car, he explains. Actually
it's a visit to the Vendôme where his father is staying. He
needs money.

"Money? My boy, certain large banks excepted, that
is the single great need common to us all."

He's a drama critic. He has a fine, sable beard, carefully trimmed. His clothes are always beautiful. He is
wearing a blue, batiste shirt that seems not to touch him
anywhere except at the neck and wrists which he is but-
toning, a shirt that encircles him with an elegant slimness.

"Money," he says. "Of course. I share that need. Listen, are you coming to dinner with us?"

He is dressing to go out with friends. They're all very
clever. Long, amusing stories, usually irreverent. The
women are as witty as the men. Saturday evening. The
small cups are refilled with coffee. The Gauloise smoke
ascends.

On the chair there are phonograph records. On the
desk, fresh books. On the bureau, three leather watch-
bands bought that day in Hermès. His father shoots his
cuffs with a slight, habitual gesture and turns to the mirror. The room is filled with the scent of his lotion, Zizanie,
which comes in cool aluminum bottles. Only his luggage
seems worn.

"Jacquette is going to be there, you haven't met
him. And Yeli Ezoum." He unrolls names like a splendid carpet.

"I can't tonight," Dean says.

"What is it, a girl? Let me see you. You look a little drawn."

"There isn't any girl."

"We're going to the Vert Bocage."

Dean is silent. Desperation is making him weak.

"Now, Phillip," his father says, "come on. This is really like climbing a ladder. Let's go up one rung at a time. First, why can't you join us for dinner?"

"Please. I can't."

"I see."

"I really need to borrow some money." It seems too abrupt.

"Oh, that's about four or five rungs farther up."

"Seriously . . ."

"Call me tomorrow," his father says, "and we'll have lunch."

"Tomorrow . . ."

"All right?"

"But I need it now," Dean pleads. He is praying.

"We'll talk about it tomorrow."

"That's too late," he says stubbornly.

"Oh, come now," his father makes it seem foolish. He is brushing the sleeves of his jacket. "Don't become so absolutely tedious. Here," and from his wallet he takes out three hundred francs.

"Now, why is it you can't come to dinner?"

For a moment Dean thinks crazily of bringing her along. Her clothes are so cheap though. The leather of her shoes is cracked. It would be awful. They would greet her with indulgent smiles, ask little questions.

"I really can't," he says.

When he gets back, finally, he finds her asleep. He lifts the edge of the covers. She is naked. He pulls off his shoes and undresses. He lies down beside her, and she rolls into his arms. Seven in the evening. The noise from the streets drifts upwards. The soft hours of early night. He reaches for the pack of *préservatifs* on the telephone stand, but she takes hold of his wrist.

"You don't need to," she says.

"Are you sure?"

"Yes."

He is overwhelmed. As his prick goes into her, he discovers the world. He knows the source of numbers, the path of the stars. Music pouring over them from somewhere, ah, from her white plastic radio. She's put a hand towel beneath her, and it becomes bloody. He finds it later. He packs it secretly when they leave.

On Sunday they walk the bridges and sometime in the early afternoon, leave town.

That night he tells me about it, not everything, of course. I'm so happy to see him, to have him confiding in me, that I miss a lot. He's worn out from the drive. In the street, dark as a ship's hull, the car is parked. The engine is still warm. Beneath the chilled body there's a faint cracking, as of joints. In the house we sit shivering. The walls are like steel. We go down to the Foy for some hot tea and cognac. By this time he's talking of other things— where to eat cheaply—I don't remember. I am hardly listening. I hear only enough to keep track of what he's saying while my real thoughts circle around us like hungry dogs.

10

What had happened? They had gone off and made love. That isn't so rare. One must expect to encounter it. It's nothing but a sweet accident, perhaps just the end of illusion. In a sense one can say it's harmless, but why, then, beneath everything does one feel so apart? Isolated. Murderous, even.

In a way I could calmly expect that from this point they would begin, having discovered all there was so soon, to lose interest in each other, to grow cold, but these acts are sometimes merely an introduction—in the great, carnal duets I think they must often be—and I search for the exact ciphers which serve to open it all as if for a safe combination. I rearrange events and make up phrases to reveal how the first innocence changed into long Sunday mornings, the bells filling the air, pillows jammed under her belly, her marvelous behind high in the daylight. Dean slowly inserts himself, deep as a sword wound.

I prefer not to think about it, I turn away, but it's impossible to control these dreams. The forbidden ones are incandescent—they burn through resolutions like cloth. I cannot stop them even if I want to. I cannot make them vanish. They are brighter than the day that surrounds me. I am weary from it. I have become a somnambulist. My own life suddenly seems nothing, an old costume, a collection of rags, and I walk, I breathe to the rhythm of his which is stronger than mine. The world is all changed. The scabs of reality are picked away and beneath them, though I try not to see, are visions which cause me to tremble.

In her room they are warming their hands at the heater. She's tired. Her work that day was hard. He undresses her, a little awkwardly, for she is still far from being his—one can imagine her still refusing—and puts her to bed. Above the thick quilt her face shines like a child's. He stands looking at her, filled with contentment. They say nothing. He adjusts the covers, which are somewhat soiled, smooths them down. Then hurriedly, as an afterthought, he takes off his clothes and slips in beside her. An act which threatens us all. The town is silent around them. On the milk-white faces of the clock the hands, in unison, jerk to new positions. The trains are running on time. Along the empty streets, yellow head-lights of a car occasionally pass and bells mark the hours, the quarters, the halves. With a touch like flowers, she is gently tracing the base of his cock, driven by now all the way into her, touching his balls, and beginning to writhe slowly beneath him in a sort of obedient rebellion while in his own dream he rises a little and defines the moist rim of her cunt with his finger, and as he does, he comes like a bull. They remain close for a long time, still without talking. It is these exchanges which cement them, that is the terrible thing. These atrocities induce them towards love.

I hear him come in. I am reading. I appear to be. Henry the Fourth is beautifying Paris, building the Place Royale, the Pont-Neuf. I keep going over the same lines again and again. I can tell what has happened, but I cannot bring myself to say anything. Nothing. I am possessed of nothing but phrases as heavy as logs.

.... *11* ....

I t is all in fragments, like the half of a paper napkin— for a time in the top drawer of his bureau—on which they both had written words. There are two columns, and I can see they were added to alternately, like a game. His is on the left. It begins with *Croix de Fer.* Opposite, in her hand: *Les Martiens.* He writes *Les Escaliers.* She writes *Le Select.* They are naming a hotel, the one they will have together someday. Dean can get the money, he says—his father knows everybody. His father has rich friends. The list continues:

Pharaoh	*Napoléon*
Les Copains	*L'Aigle Noir*
Le Pyramide	*Quatre Saisons*
Coco	*Moderne*

and the bottom is missing, like a letter torn apart on the wet street.

It is in Nancy, in the hotel on the square. A bright December afternoon. In the center of everything, the statue of Stanislas, traces of old snow at his feet, his green arm pointing to the barren park. They are ushered into the silence of a room on the side. She is happy. It is the weekend. They have wandered along the street in the great, plain-faced crowd, and she has seen a leather suit that costs 130 francs which she imagines he may buy for her. She was wearing a black fur hat. Every eye followed when she walked.

The radio is playing. They undress in the winter daylight. Dean is a little embarrassed at his condition. His prick gets hard whenever he looks at her. He can't help it. His chief desire is to raise her on it, exultant, to run her up into the sunshine, into the starlight where she can see the world. They begin to dance a little, naked, in the early darkness, the music thin and foreign, their feet bare on the rug. Then they make love, she astride him, in the favorite manner of the Roman poets, as he informs her. He lies gazing up at her, his hands encircling her ankles. The rich smell of her falls over him. At the bottom of it all, his eyes lingering there, the mute triangle in which he is implanted.

"Do you think you will remember me in five years?" she asks him at dinner.

He tries to smile, but it's dry. He is empty, with no desire to talk about love.

"You will go," she says. "You are the type."

"No."

"*Si*," she insists calmly.

By now they know something of each other. There is a fund they can draw on together. The encounter begins to have an essence of its own which neither can define but which nourishes them both, and happily, in the single unselfish ritual of love, they contribute to it all they can. Nor does it matter how much either takes away. It is a limitless body. It can never be exhausted but only, although one never believes this, forgot.

They are served a dish piled high with *écrevisses*, salty, pale. The tiny legs crack like dry wood under their teeth. The hidden juices spurt. She wants to know what they are called. Dean isn't sure. Crayfish, he says.

"Crayfish?"

"I think so," he says.

She invents a story: The Prince of Crayfish. Dean listens, licking his fingers while she unfolds, as if to a child, a tale filled with mysteries.

Deep down, where it is only darkness, the prince of crayfish was born. It was very difficult. It took a long time because his feet kept getting tangled up with his mother's, but finally he was swimming, a little weakly, by her side. From all over the sea important fish came to bring him presents: necklaces of coral, little moules to to eat, seaweed to lie on, green and black . . .

He is watching her mouth, her clever eyes. Her teeth are a bad color and not well cared for. One can see that when she smiles, but he is only watching the phrases, he hardly notices.

When he was six months old, he said to his mother: I am going up to see the world. Ah, she was very sad. She cried. She didn't want, but then she said: God be with you, my dear son. Be brave and honest and no hurt will . . .

"Befall you," Dean supplies, as if in a dream.

"Befall you," she says, the word funny in her mouth. "No hurt will befall you."

"Go on," he says.

"Do you like it?"

"Oh, yes."

From waters so deep he had to swim for three days before it even began to grow light, he makes his way to the surface . . .

An odyssey which ends—Dean is shocked—in disaster, in a great, frothing kettle where the prince is scalded to death, still brave, still honest . . . She shrugs over the soup at the abruptness of it all. Dean sits silent. He is drained of all invention and also aware, for the first time, that she is fully able to speak, to create images strong enough to alter his life.

They return to the hotel at ten. The corridors are empty. Shoes are set outside each room. The catch of the door makes a little click as it closes and with that sound, Dean suddenly awakes. He turns the bolt. They are safe. The city is his. No one in it is more powerful. Hushed in sleep it lies, white specks of frost on its windows, steeped in the cold. No one is more blessed, more demonic.

In the bathroom she stands naked before the thin mirror. Dean appears behind her. His hands, all reverence at first, like those of men reprieved, move to possess her. Tenderly he weighs her breasts.

"I would look very well in that suit," she reflects.

With no resonance, he says, *"Oui."*

"This one grew first," she says.

"Is that true?" Dean says inanely.

"He was always bigger. *Oui.*"

He becomes attentive to the smaller.

"Poor baby," he murmurs.

Above the basin on a glass shelf: her bottles. Biodop, one of them reads. Her stockings lie crumpled on the floor. Over the radio: *Nights of Spain*. The suit, he remembers, had a belt which was a gleaming, leather thong.

They have turned off the light. In the room there is a huge *armoire*, a wicker basket, chairs. A metal tree on which garments can be hung. The ceiling is very high. In its center—one's eyes must become accustomed to the dark—a grotesque fixture. The hours pass. She is pinioned on the bed, her arms trapped beneath her, her legs forced wide. Her eyes are closed. The radio is playing *Sucu Sucu*. The world has stopped. Oceans still as photographs. Galaxies floating down. Her cunt tastes sweet as fruit.

Morning. She lies face down, warm still from sleep. Her arms are up on either side of her head, the elbows bent. Dean is on top of her, encircling, in the early light, and they are fucking like weight lifters. He pauses at last. He leans over to admire her, she does not see him. Hair covers her cheek. Her skin seems very white. He kisses her side and then, without force, as one stirs a favorite mare, begins again. She comes to life with a soft, exhausted sound, like someone saved from drowning.

Her narrow, cool back commanding the breakfast. The waiter who brings it does not even glance towards the bed. When he is gone she jumps up and, still naked, prepares the trays. In the noiseless light she opens the *croissants*, diligent as a maid, spreads them evenly with butter, arranges them back on the plates. Her flesh shines. It draws him. He moves to stay near her, like a child, hoping she will smile at him, give him a taste. He feels like jumping around, making noise, she is so occupied, so serene. She opens the *confiture*. Put some here, he wants to say. Grab her around the waist. Dance. He kisses her elbow. She glances at him and smiles.

Place Stanislas on a still Sunday morning. Windows through which the silence of Nancy pours, borne by the pure light. It is in this city that she was born, in one melancholy autumn of the war. Her father had already left home to live with his mistress. Her mother was alone. A cold winter that year, a snowy winter, hard as stone, ice gleaming in the sunshine along the roofs. A winter which somehow formed her though she could not speak as much as a single word.

The remains of breakfast lie littered about like a feast from the night before. Across the street is the opera, touches of gold on the balcony railing, posters invisible below. *Lucie de Lammermoor* will be here, dark letters printed on violet. *La Vie Bohème.* They have gone back to bed and lie almost enclosed in a second sleep, the radio weak, her fingers lightly, the skin draws tight beneath them, tracing his balls.

In the bathroom he watches her putting up her hair. Her arms are raised. In the hollows there is a shadow of growth, short and soft, and to this belongs a damp, oniony odor which he loves. When she is in the tub, he begins to scrub her back. She complains. It's too hard.

He runs his fingertips lightly over the skin.

"It looks better," he says.

She does not reply. She is bent forward slightly in the thin, comforting steam, her arms along the white rim. Beneath them, faintly commonplace, her breasts are visible, as if he might see them any time he liked, as if they were ordinary as knees. The palest nipples—he can barely see one. He kneels there beside the tub. She begins to wash her legs.

Simple moments of immodesty, an immodesty which finishes desire, one often hears, in a great and abiding city. I have visited and read a good deal about Nancy. The capital of Lorraine. A model of eighteenth-century planning. Its harmonious squares, its elegant houses are typically French and appropriate to so rich a region, but its glory it owes to a Pole, Stanislas Leszczynski, who was given the duchies of Lorraine and Bar by his son-in-law, Louis XV, and who ruled from Nancy which he devoted himself to embellishing. An ancient city. The old quarter has never been altered. A city of rich merchants, strategic, key to the lands along the border. In front of its very walls ... But how flat this all seems, how hopeless, like a cheap backdrop shaking as the actors walk.

12

Sunday mornings. Gloved hands touching, they drive along the empty boulevard. Schools are closed. The iron gates are locked in front of those long, damp alleys smelling of pee. A watery sunshine, blenched by skies which refuse to warm, falls on the blocks and corners. Unexpectedly, like a band of survivors, there is a crowd, all decently dressed, just leaving church. They squint as they come out into the light. They leave the steps, walk along, stop at the baker's for bread. From there they scatter, the warm loaves under their arms.

Dean is a little bored. It's an effort to speak French. He's weary of it, and English is no better, hers is so uneven. Her mistakes begin to be irritating, and besides, she seems disposed to talk only of banal things: shoes, her work at the office. When she is silent, he glances at her and smiles. She doesn't respond. She senses it, he thinks. Suddenly, he feels transparent. The eyes that return his somewhat mechanical glance are the eyes of a knowing child, and all the evasions, poses, devices become foolish. The windshield has faint streaks of blue like air. As he looks through, at the road ahead, he is conscious of her calm appraisal. She understands effortlessly. Life is all quite clear to her. She is one with it. She moves in it like a fish, never wondering if it has a bottom, shores, worlds above it . . .

Worlds below. Those provincial Sundays I walked along the streets on the way perhaps to lunch with the Jobs, encountering as I went, even inventing myself, those small epiphanies of which the town is comprised. The clink of spoons as they dine, unseen, behind the shutters of the girls' school. The graveled courts, the gardens of Autun. I stood near the window as I dressed, steeped in aching thoughts and hoping for the appearance, even for a moment emerging from her door, of Claude Picquet. Icicles fall from the roof, broken free by sunlight, and flash past the window. She never comes out. The street remains still. As I look back, I see that life is like a game of solitaire and every once in a while there is a move. Despite it all, I could have been happy, a quiet happiness to be sure, but happy nonetheless. I could have found it very pleasant to walk into town if the weather were nice— things like that. It is knowledge that poisons us, events one would hesitate to imagine.

Winter days remarkable only for their calm . . . I go down to the Café Français and sit with my back to the mirrors watching them play cards. I have beautiful shots of this, many reflected in the glass. The camera was in my lap, sometimes behind a newspaper. The click of the shutter was softer than a match strike. The waitress pretending not to see. People come in the door, which is right on the corner. One wall is all windows on the square. The light is flooding but mild. The voices are low. I spread out the newspaper and begin to read. Occasionally I make some notes.

Of course, there's Paris. I stand waiting on the *quai* in the icy dark. The clock shines white as the moon. The early train is an adventure, rocking along as dawn comes, rushing through villages of the dead. I take a seat at the end of the car. All the compartments look stuffy, thick with the odors of sleep. It's after nine when we pull into Nevers. There's a clatter of doors. Bursts of cold air from outside. A handsome girl boards wearing a checkered coat. Her father is there to see her off, I watch him through the windows. He is waiting rather diffidently for the train to begin moving and then, as it does, he shows a last, hurried affection. She has the scars of some skin disease on her cheeks, otherwise an intelligent face. And she has good legs and hands. Her father looked quite distinguished.

After we are moving she comes out of her compartment and enters the *cabinet-toilette,* just behind me. She passes very close in a red silk suit. She has a nice figure. A long time passes. I begin to be uneasy. I don't know why. I begin to become aware of myself sitting innocently at the end of the passage. Silence, except for the train. Finally I hear paper tearing. The sound alarms me. We are passing dead engines. Farther down the car, two men are standing, one in the thick, blue uniform of the French Air Force. More paper tearing. They're paying no attention to me, absolutely none, but suddenly I'm afraid. I have a moment of agonizing premonition. She's going to do something terrible, burst out, wipe shit on my face, abuse me, screaming things I know I won't be able to understand. I am about to stand up and move when there are explosions of air as we pass more engines. The sound is terrifying.

And then the great, blackened terminal in Paris, that filthy cathedral, stale and exhausted, through which one passes into grey, commercial streets. I walk outside to find a cab, falling wearily into the back seat although it's only a little past noon. I am thinking of Cristina who later, as we drive to dinner, will begin to tell me about Isabel's husband who comes to her now for advice. They're very friendly. They drive around town talking while he off-handedly points to various buildings he owns.

"Fabulous apartment houses," she says, shrugging up her shoulders in helplessness. She is in an expensive black dress from which her neck emerges quite bare.

"He didn't own that one," Billy says. "It was the little, tiny one next door."

"The little one next door," she agrees. "Yes. All right. But he's shown me lots of others."

"Well, I just wouldn't believe everything he says."

"I don't know," she says. "Why not?"

"I just wouldn't," Billy says. "You know, I talk to a lot of people."

"He's marvelous," she says to me. "Believe me. Crazy about art."

She's had a few drinks already, bad for her liver, of course. She knows it, she won't be able to sleep. Then she'll begin to get terrible attacks, especially because of the not sleeping. Billy says that's right: she ought to rest more.

We go to Chez Noé, just along the river, where as soon as we appear, we are embraced with cries of joy. They haven't been here for months—it's the place they used to come to before they were married.

"When we were sleeping together," Cristina says.

Billy glances at her.

A small restaurant, plain as an aunt's house. Upstairs it's relatively empty. They put us by the window. Cristina insists on champagne.

"I feel like it tonight."

"Watch out, Bummy," he says.

She gives a foolish laugh.

"All right," he says. "Remember, I told you."

"Yes, darling," she says.

Outside I can see the black river, battered like foil, and the Wheatlands' tan Mercedes abandoned under the streetlights, nosed in, not exactly parallel with the curb. Cristina's a painter, or more exactly would have been a painter if it weren't for her first marriage. She laid it all aside for that. With Billy it's been different. She's attending classes again, but . . . she sighs.

"No," he assures her, "the paintings you're doing now are the best you've ever done. You've even said that yourself."

"I don't know, they've gotten too intellectual," she says. "All the life has suddenly gone out of them."

"No, it hasn't."

"You're not a painter," she says. Then to me, "Lend me your handkerchief."

For a moment I'm afraid she's going to cry, but she merely blows her nose. She looks directly at me. Her smiles are always mysterious.

"Tell him who's in your class, now," Billy says.

Isabel. She arrives with her poodle and ties the leash to one leg of the easel. She's very serious about her work, she won't joke about it.

"Is she a good painter?" I ask.

"You don't know how funny you are," Cristina says. Her flesh is lambent against the black of her dress, and she seems full of those rebellious acts that come to her so naturally when she drinks. She has large, lovely eyes and pale lashes. "There's no one in that whole class who can paint. Well, just one. Alix could be a good painter, but she won't work. You have to be willing to give up everything."

"Of course."

"I mean it," she tells me. "Do you know Alix?"

"I don't think so."

"She's divine," Cristina says. "You'd like her."

The owners sit down with us, Michelle first, approaching with a lovely smile. She's not young, but rather in the midst of that last and most confident beauty, like the mother of a schoolmate. You see her emerging from a car, the flash of an elegant calf, and you are tumbled into unbearable love.

Michelle has a surprise: she and Charles have been married! Amid the congratulations and sincere embraces, Charles enters sheepishly, and this sets off another wave of salutes. They open more champagne and even bring out the reserve Calvados. Afterwards, they sing a little duet together. It's quite touching. Through the many years she spent as his mistress, they were perfectly open about their relationship, but marriage causes them to blush and tell jokes. Michelle's son, who is fifteen or so, comes upstairs with a friend. Everybody sits around and talks with the exception of the friend and me. We are strangers to the past that unites them. The friend smokes cigarettes, and I drink the Calvados.

When we leave, there's an argument, the second of the night. The first was when Cristina wouldn't go down to the garage with him to get the car. Now he wants to go dancing.

"Oh, God," she says.

"God, what?" He always becomes sullen.

"Nobody goes dancing," she says.

Instead we go to a *cave*. Billy is angry and bored the whole time. There's a negress who sings in beautiful French, her sequin dress glittering with the brilliance of crystal scales. She is like a naiad in a skin of silver. Her teeth are hypnotic. Her smile crushes one's hope. Billy is watching her impassively. Cristina leans on my shoulder and reveals I'm the only friend of his, the only one, she likes.

"You ought to be a painter," she tells me, "you know?"

"You think so?"

"Yes. I mean, we're doing the same thing, aren't we? You and I."

"Not exactly. I don't change anything."

"Of course you do!" she says fiercely.

"No, I don't think so. Anyway, it doesn't matter that much, I couldn't be a painter. *You* ought to be a painter."

She smiles strangely. I am afraid to explain.

"You're so right," she finally says. She notices Billy. "Baby," she says, "what's wrong?"

"Nothing," he replies coldly.

She laughs.

"Let's go dancing," she says.

We drive along Boulevard Raspail. There's a club somewhere, hidden among the ordinary storefronts. They can't agree where it is until suddenly we are going past it. Billy stops with a jerk. He backs into a parking place with ferocious skill. Cristina gets out and takes my arm. This is a place the Greek shipping millionaires come to, she tells me. The band never stops.

Cristina refuses to dance, of course. We watch the others instead, a sleek Japanese girl who's been sitting at the bar and a man of sixty, fat as a pastry cook. They part in rhythm and face the side. Then they dance back to back. He's absurd, but very graceful. His feet are nimble as mice. Finally they begin playing something Cristina likes. We dance with her in turn.

"Onassis sits at that table over there," she tells me out on the floor.

"Which?"

"In the corner."

"Oh." I stare at it. "What does he look like?"

"You've seen pictures of him, haven't you?" she says.

"Yes, but I mean close up . . ."

"He looks very rich," she says.

"Does he wear those tinted glasses?"

"You mean sunglasses? All of them do. You never know what they're thinking."

"About you, I imagine."

"Me?" she says.

"I'm sure he has an appreciative eye."

"I'd like to catch it sometime."

"Would you really marry a rich man?"

"Next time," she says. "Oh, it wouldn't last, but he'd be very happy."

"Would he?"

"Oh, yes," she promises.

She has her moments. Still, it's dangerous to believe in what she seems to be. One often has the impression there is another, desperate woman underneath, but this is the extent of her power, this intimation of sexual wealth. Billy always talks about how beautiful she is. It's almost as if he's protesting: but she *is* beautiful. And she is. Their life is arranged to exhibit this beauty. They treat it like the possession of a fine house.

A tall, enraptured dancer, dark as a gypsy, comes onto the floor. He's in a business suit. His hair is long, and his shoes have high, leather heels. There's the glitter of madness about him as he dances alone, the friends at his table watching with smiles. The Japanese girl can see him. The fat man can hear his feet. The music continually quickens. A regular contest has begun. It's like the start of a crime of passion, they are already winding the shroud around the poor, fat bourgeois, hot glances meeting as they writhe on either side. But he will not die. He dances like a man possessed, his face flushed and shining with sweat, his mouth in a dead man's smile. Now it drops open. Everything in the club has stopped. Everybody is watching. Any second I expect to see him crumple like an old coat. The music alone can kill him. They are dancing in a frenzy. The musicians have gone wild.

On the way home we get lost. Even though they've lived in the city for five years, Billy doesn't know where we are. There's no one to ask. We slow down at the corners to try and read the plaques and then, tires scorching, take off. The streets are empty except for an occasional car. Even the big intersections. We race around for an hour. Cristina's head lies limply on my shoulder. She's sleeping. After a while—we are going by certain stores for the third time—she begins to sing. Her eyes are still closed. Slurred, faintly poetic phrases come from her mouth. Billy glances at her. He seems like the doctor driving us to a hospital. Finally, just as we come into a part of town he recognizes, she struggles up. I feel a sudden disappointment, as if she's abandoned me, but then in return, with a sure instinct she shows me the truest of smiles. We are passing various galleries. She watches them go by.

"There," she points out. "That's where I'm going to have a showing some day. Right in that gallery."

We're looking through the rear window now.

"That one?"

"The best gallery in Paris."

Billy ignores her. She begins to arrange her hair, turning the rearview mirror so she can see herself. He says nothing. She begins to stroke his collar. The sky has lost its blackness. It's too late to sleep.

My bed is in a room which also serves as the study. It's just off the stairway. One has to pass through it to get to theirs. Enormous drapes, almost too heavy to swell, are drawn across the windows, but already it seems the bottoms are edged by a faint light. Sunday morning. I close my eyes and wait. Perhaps we'll have breakfast at one o'-clock or so. Afterwards we may do something amusing.

13

They are waiting on the street in the late afternoon. The air is thin as paper. The day is raw. Anne-Marie's girl friend is supposed to come. Of course, he's curious even though he pretends he's not. He wants to see what she's like. He glances around, trying to pick her out from afar. Finally she appears, in a coat with a little fur collar, complaining about the cold. A grocer's daughter from St. Léger. Her name is Danielle.

In the café Dean sits idly while they talk in French. Danielle seems older, more assured. She has long hair which she wears loose and keeps stroking smoothly as she talks. He glances through her notebook. It's school work. The pages are graph paper. Pale blue rulings, neat equations, proofs. After a while he is aware she is watching. He closes the book.

They say goodbye at the door, she has to catch the train.

"*A toute à l'heure,*" Dean says.

"No," she corrects him abruptly. "You don't see me later, not today. It's *à bientôt.*"

"*A bientôt,*" he says.

Afterwards, Anne-Marie asks if he liked her. Dean doesn't answer.

"She has nice hair," he says.

"Her mother doesn't let her cut it."

"No?"

They sit in silence. He is still annoyed. And it's disturbing to suddenly find she has another life, someone else she wants to see. He orders a glass of wine. He asks if she would like one. She seems very quiet.

"No," she says, "*merci.*"

They have a light dinner down near the station. The waiter there knows them. Not many people come in on winter evenings, and they sit alone in the long, reflecting room and talk in low voices. A solitary car turns past the square. Without daring to look at him, she touches his idle hand. Then slowly, taking heart, she begins to stroke his fingers one by one.

In the room she begs him to undress her. He does it lifelessly. It's very cold. She hurries into bed.

"Do you want me to slip in beside you for a while?" he says at last.

"You don't have to ask me that."

Quickly he pulls off his clothes, his flesh tightening as the chilly sheets enclose it. They both lie still, waiting for the warmth of their bodies to permit them to touch. There is the whisper of her arm as she reaches up.

"I love your hair," she says.

Dean is silent.

"Do you like it?"

He shrugs.

"Oh . . ." he says.

"It's very soft. It's like seal," she says.

"Seal?"

"Yes. *Beaux cheveux*," she murmurs. She surrenders to the name. "*Beaux cheveux.*"

These whispered words overcome him. He turns his head to face her in the dark. Their mouths meet. Her breath is thin and rotten. It makes him dizzy. It makes him long for air. There is light from the crack under the door, a light which slowly reveals the room. He can make out her clear, her saintly face now, pale as a letter. Through the wall come the weak voices of people next door. Otherwise the silence is complete. They can no longer hear the heater or the clock, the sound of an occasional truck. They have proceeded into themselves. Her hand touches his chest and begins to fall in excruciating, slow designs. He lies still as a dog beneath it, still as an idiot.

She was seduced at seventeen by an Italian waiter in Contrexéville. It was her first summer away from home. She knew no one. She was not going to resist. Every night she went to dance, with another girl or alone, and she met him there in the conversation and cheap scents of the pavilion. She liked him, but the summer ended. He was gone. Of course, in Orléans she was quickly discovered, and there was Roland in Troyes, and his friends, boys in St. Léger, Citroens parked in the dense woods, young Tunisians working as salesmen. Dean knows he's not the first. But he has no inclination to wonder, at least not about that, for neither is he entirely what he seems. Intelligent, yes, but somehow he is weary of his gifts. Already he seems to be outliving them. He sometimes thinks otherwise, but he's finished with school. The clever mathematician is disappearing, the young man for whom everything was too easy. His existence is already becoming clouded, strange. He is like a son who has been cut off and now is discarding the customs, the course of ordinary life without hesitation, with all the assurance of an anarchist.

His mother is dead. She was a suicide. Her marriage was terrifying to her. In the center of it she found herself completely alone. During the last year she sent long telegrams to her sister, sometimes quoting poetry, Swinburne, Blake. One day she burned her diaries, a spring day, and walked into the Connecticut River to drown, just like Virginia Woolf or Madame Magritte. She was buried in Boston, her home. I could see the ceremony. Dean is six years old and his sister three. They stand stunned and obedient as the great, glistening coffin is lowered into the ground. Within lies the drowned woman who had given them life and who now gives an example of melancholy and commitment which will stay with them forever. Clods of earth thunder onto the hollow lid and, half-orphan, bearer of his mother's death which is not yet even real, he begins his life. Much of it you know, at any rate college, the wanderings.

Now, at twenty-four, he has come to the time of choice. I know quite well how all that is. And then, I read his letters. His father writes to him in the most beautiful, educated hand, the born hand of a copyist. Admonitions to confront life, to think a little more seriously about this or that. I could have laughed. Words that meant nothing to him. He has already set out on a dazzling voyage which is more like an illness, becoming ever more distant, more legendary. His life will be filled with those daring impulses which cause him to disappear and next be heard of in Dublin, in Veracruz . . . I am not telling the truth about Dean, I am inventing him. I am creating him out of my own inadequacies, you must always remember that.

After a while, the second phase begins: the time of few choices. Uncertainties, strange fears of the past. Finally, of course, comes the third phase, the closing, and one must begin shutting out the world as if by panels because the strength to consider everything in all its shattering diversity is gone and the shape of life—but he will be in a poet's grave by then—finally appears, like a drop about to fall.

Dean doesn't quite understand this yet. It doesn't mean anything in particular to him. He is, after all, not discontented. Her breasts are hard. Her cunt is sopping. He fucks her gracefully, impelled by pure joy. He arches up to see her and to look at his prick plunging in, his balls tight beneath it. Mythology has accepted him, images he cannot really believe in, images brief as dreams. The sweat rolls down his arms. He tumbles into the damp leaves of love, he rises clean as air. There is nothing about her he does not adore. When they are finished, she lies quiet and limp, exhausted by it all. She has become entirely his, and they lie like drunkards, their bare limbs crossed. In the cold distance the bells begin, filling the darkness, clear as psalms.

14

Saturday, the sixth of January. The sky is cloudless, blue, cold as ice and yet burning the eyes. The sun is just weak enough to be felt through the windshield, no more. It's the coldest day of the year. He takes a curve on the wrong side near Beaune and then, too late, sees the figure near the edge of the trees, a figure in uniform who casually waves him down, now it is two of them: *gendarmes.* Dean has crossed the solid line in the middle of the road. It's quite serious. In France the *agents* don't fool around. One doesn't misbehave. Slowly they walk across to the car. They have the faces of hunters, unemotional and wise. They ask for his papers. His French vanishes. It crumbles to a few, inept words. He stammers and can answer only with difficulty. The policemen are patient. They seem to be watching his mouth, as if they might understand him despite himself. Not more than a glance on their part at Anne-Marie who sits still as a housemaid while Dean struggles and lies. It seems the ordeal will never end. Finally they deliver a warning, with gestures, and allow him to go on. Dean thanks them.

He knows he's been a fool. It's made even more clear by her silence, by something in her face. He behaved like a frightened boy. Worse, he couldn't even find words.

"It's lucky I don't speak French that well," he says, forcing a laugh.

"*Oui,*" she says.

All the way to Dijon she is somewhat disinterested in him. They ride in an unbroken silence, the cold leaking in on them, the whole day blue with it, people, objects, the very light. He pulls up before the Hôtel de la Cloche.

"What do you think of it?"

She doesn't reply.

It's only when the door of the room is opened that she suddenly changes.

"*Ah!*" she cries, "*c'est très jolie!*"

Dean is suspicious. It's ridiculously modern. The corridors they walked along were built to grand dimensions, suitably gloomy, and now this: loud colors and the bareness of new furniture. The floor has been scraped and varnished. The yellow wallpaper is printed with hundreds of small, colored balls. He wonders if she's being sarcastic, but no, she begins to unpack happily. She looks into the bathroom. She finds it perfect. Dean is annoyed. A wave of uncertainty comes over him. The afternoon begins to seem ominous. It has an emptiness he suddenly cannot think how to fill.

"Do we go out?" she says.

"Jesus, it's bitter cold."

"*Pardon?*"

"It's too cold," he says. "Where do you want to go?"

She shrugs. To see the stores.

"It's freezing," he says.

"*Non,*" she complains.

The streets are crowded, cold weather or not. They walk around until six, looking in windows, and before one good shop stand a long time admiring a black pullover. Suddenly he decides to buy it for her. They go inside. It costs forty francs. It's more than he thought. The *vendeuse* waits, her face expressionless. It seems they are all listening. The pullover lies limp, a fine label gleaming within its throat. Forty francs. Finally he nods.

"All right," he says. It's like throwing away the oars.

She clings to his arm as they walk along afterwards, and he sees their reflection in the chilly glass. They look like a working couple. He is thin, tough, no necktie. It's evening. He imagines he looks like a boxer.

The faint warmth of the hotel room restores him. She begins to strip off her clothes like a roommate and climb into bed. Dean undresses, too. He takes off his shoes. He unbuttons his shirt slowly, with the assurance of an athlete.

It is almost dark. Her arms are caught beneath her. He feels her hesitate, then begin to surrender. In the dusk, her desperate spasms fill him with the deepest, the most profound joy.

They have dinner on the rue Michelet, in a restaurant filled with the soft clatter of plates, a long dinner that seems almost a reminiscence they are so pleased, so content to eat in silence. They look up to find themselves exchanging smiles. At the end they become sleepy. They stuff themselves with cheese, *époisses*, *citeaux*, specialties of a region known for its food.

She cannot be satisfied. She will not let him alone. She removes her clothes and calls to him. Once that night and twice the next morning he complies and in the darkness between lies awake, the lights of Dijon faint on the ceiling, the boulevards still. It's a bitter night. Flats of rain are passing. Heavy drops ring in the gutter outside their window, but they are in a dovecote, they are pigeons beneath the eaves. The rain is falling all around them. Deep in feathers, breathing softly, they lie. His sperm swims slowly inside her, oozing out between her legs.

The wine has made him thirsty. At about three in the morning he gets up for water. She turns her head sleepily and asks for some, too. She rises on one elbow to drink it. His hand supports her back. Afterwards he opens the window wider. The rain is steady, hard as pellets. He can hear it falling on the roofs of Dijon, shifting, moving then in a different direction, across the avenues, down the black streets. He would like to kiss her behind the knees. At last he sleeps.

He will never awaken, not from this dream, that much I know. He is already too deep. He has reached the nadir. He cannot move. In the morning, in the clear, holy light he moves like an affectionate father, drawing her to him and pulling the pillows down.

15

She was conceived after much difficulty—I do not know if this is significant—and born in the fall of 1944, the last autumn of the war. Her father had already been gone for two months. Her mother, whom I shall never see, had a poor, unhappy life, even though she eventually married again. There is a winter in which her child is sick, a depressing winter. She struggles through it alone. The restaurants are lighted. Behind the flat, steamy windows of the Café du Commerce businessmen are talking. The pale, neon script of the dance hall sign illuminates a narrow court—as she passes, coming home from the hospital in the evening darkness, she can see the couples enter. Her fingers are cold, her feet. Her life has no solution. It is like a crime that cannot be undone.

I don't know how to think of this mother, this uncomplaining woman I am so inclined to like. I picture her as a little plain and fond of gossip. I'm not even sure where she was born, in Metz, I think, one with Toul and Verdun of the three old bishoprics. There's no reason to say Metz, but one must place it somewhere.

Edouard, the father, was something of a dandy, although as he grew older he became stout. He was born in Belgium. Anne-Marie sees him from time to time. He lives in the sunshine of later years (he was considerably older than her mother) with a young wife north of Paris. She has a job as he's not able to work too much any more. He has a few investments, and they're able to get by. He's very careful with his money, even more than most French, which is in itself quite something. They have a little boy eleven years old. The surprising thing is that Anne-Marie and her mother both think fondly of this villain. The mother has even gone so far as to keep the little boy for a few weeks while Edouard and his wife were off in Scandinavia. Of course, she was paid something, but still it seems extraordinary. As for her present husband, I know nothing about him, nothing at all. He's saved her from a lonely life; that's it.

There's a photograph of Annie and her father and stepbrother, the three of them looking directly at the camera. She is sixteen but seems younger. Behind them is what appears to be the railroad station, large windows, distinguished façade. It's one of those ordinary little snapshots which illustrate the life of almost everybody. It was taken in the sunshine. Their faces are blazing white, their eyes are narrowed. The only exceptional thing about it is her presence which makes one pick it up and look closely to see if she had already become anything at that age, if there is something in her face . . . She keeps it in the *armoire*, propped up so it can be seen when the door is opened. Just behind it is a small, cardboard box and in that, two or three hundred francs, her savings. Dean knows the money is there. He's seen her put some in. She sends part of her pay to her mother, but the existence of that thin sheaf of bank notes, a couple of months' rent is all it amounts to, is somehow touching. I see it there like the motive for a betrayal, but of course, it's just the opposite. Still, it's remarkable that it should be there, so lightly hidden. She is careful about money. She is humorless about it. She never spends any when she is with him. Perhaps she might buy some postage stamps, nothing more. She has never bought him a gift of any kind, at least not that I know of. And still, with the stale taste of poverty all around her, I am certain Dean could have those two hundred francs if he asked for them. I am terrified that he could. It seems she is ready to give too much—I am haunted by the idea—and like a fool hastening to introduce all the tedious concerns of his own life into hers, I want to warn her. On the other hand, I know there's not the slightest chance he could ever be made to take it. Or perhaps he would do so without a qualm, as if he were entitled to it just as he is to her person, her thoughts, her very dreams. I am sure of one of the two things, but I can't decide which. The money distracts me. That small, tea-colored box about the size a wristwatch might come in, with the photograph leaning against it—I can actually see it through walls of stone.

Objects have their shape and weight, their color, and beyond this a dimension for which there is no scale, their importance, and her room, her life about which I really know so little, are furnished with articles that have gradually become surreal. They appear wherever I look. They steal the identity of things that actually surround me. There is her clock which has luminous hands, which runs a little slow, a clock she had in Orléans, perhaps, in Contrex, the alarm going off early, shrill. No, there she was awakened by another girl. Summer mornings. She has been out late and is sleepy. On the floor her shoes have fallen over. Her dress has been tossed on a chair . . . There is her washcloth, sewn in the shape of a glove. Her cosmetics. Her comb. The box where her savings lie hidden. Oh, Anne-Marie, your existence is so pure. You have your poor childhood, postcards from boys in St. Léger, your stepfather, your despair. Nothing can affect you, no revelation, no crime. You are like a sad story, like leaves in the street. You repeat yourself like a song.

Dean sees her almost every night. Sometimes they don't bother to eat. An orange. A cup of tea. They drive around in the cold. In the room she undresses him and puts him to bed. He submits like a huge child. She pours a glass of wine and sets it near him. Then leisurely, as if alone, she removes her clothing and puts on a robe. She washes. She begins to brush her hair. The cloth clings to her body, Dean can make out her hips, her round buttocks. She wants a room that has carpets and mirrors, she tells him. Dean is silent. She slips out of the robe and stands naked before the mirror. And a large bed, she adds, looking at herself. He barely listens. His eyes are drifting slowly between substance and reflection. She turns to see if he is awake.

"Phillip?"

There is no answer. She approaches the bed. His hands rise silently in the dark to receive her, to draw her down.

"Pretending you are asleep," she says. "You are a naughty child."

"No."

He has turned her over to admire her, those pale cheeks, firm as calves. He caresses her, slips his hand between her legs.

"It's nourishing," he says.

"Comment?"

"Je t'aime," he says.

They lie on their sides. The clock is ticking. The metal of the heater cracks like glass. Downstairs the Corsicans are talking. Their passionate voices echo through the stairwell. The street door closes.

"Wait a minute," he whispers.
She is on top of him.
"I don't have anything."
"It's all right," she says.
"Are you sure?"
She is struggling. He is in agony.
"Anne-Marie?"
"*Si!*" she insists. He half releases her, half guides.

It begins slowly, his hands on her waist. It seems he is crowning his life.

16

Past and haunting images of France, reflected over and over again like facets of an inexhaustible stone. I walk through the silent house, the tall rooms chilled with winter light, the furnishings crossed by it, the windows. The quality of stillness is everywhere. There is no single detail that provides it. It exists like a veiled face.

Images of the towns. Sens. The famous cathedral which is reflected in the splendor of Canterbury itself rises over the icy river, over the still streets. One sees it in the distance, St. Etienne: the centuries have bleached its stone like powder and the heads are all missing from statues of the blessed, but still it appears from far off to warn travelers of the presence of God. Built as one of the first of a great, Gothic family that rose throughout France, it endures like a white myth. The little shops have grown close around it, cinemas, restaurants. Still, it cannot be touched. Beneath the noon sun the roof, which is typically Burgundian, gleams in the strange design of snakeskin, banded into diamonds, black and green, ocher, red. The sun splashes it like water. The brilliance seems to spread.

Sens. They have fallen asleep. Dean wakes first, in the early afternoon. He unfastens her stockings and slowly rolls them off. Her skirt is next and then her underpants. She opens her eyes. The garter belt he leaves on, to confirm her nakedness. He rests his head there. After a while, finding a more comfortable position, he lies between her legs, her pelvis for a pillow, her knees within his grasp. He listens to the traffic. He turns his head a little to see if she is asleep. She is looking down at him calmly. Beneath his ear it is wet.

He has money, everything is changed. There are close to nine hundred francs in immaculate bills from the sale of his return ticket on the airlines, the beauty of bank notes being counted made him weak. He didn't fold them. He carried them out flat, in the stiff packets of ten pinned at the corner. He can speak the language suddenly with them in his possession. He can see himself clearly, he can think of many things. They are important, these inexhaustible ten-franc notes. They are the essence of invention. They are the warrants of his life.

In the restaurant they arrive a little early. The tables are empty, the headwaiter is standing alone. They are led past a fireplace where a huge log is slowly burning, the flames no bigger than one's hand. On a broad table, great hams reveal their rich interiors, plates of cooked fishes, mushrooms, adornings of fruit. They are seated in a booth across from one another. She is touching a fever blister on her chin.

"Do we take the *prix-fixe?*" she asks.

"I don't know," he says. He is reading.

She keeps touching herself.

"Stop that."

She obeys.

In the next booth an elegant trio is arriving: a man with silvery hair, a perfectly groomed, well-born man and two women, his wife and mother probably. Dean can see them behind her head, they are accepting the menus. The headwaiter talks to them. They smile. He looks down again.

"Are you very hungry?" he says.

"*Ah, oui.*"

"It's an enormous dinner." His head is still down. "I don't even think you can eat it all."

"*Oh, j'ai faim,*" she pleads.

"All right."

In back of her they are conversing warmly in a splendid French of which he can hear not a word. His glances are long, too long, but he cannot withhold them. He feels himself becoming sullen. She turns to see what he is looking at, and Dean is suddenly filled with humiliation. She begins to do something beneath the table, to pick at her fingernails which have remnants of polish.

"Please," he says.

She glances up. There are terrible moments in which one sees love with cold eyes. Her face is a shopgirl's, Dean can see it plainly, pretty but cheap. He is overwhelmed with impatience. He wants only to be gone from here. They have somehow made him into a delinquent. Anne-Marie says nothing. She can smell his anger. Her hands are hidden in her lap.

They eat slowly, finding little to say. The meal is too big. She loses her appetite and cannot finish, which only annoys him more, and he eats her dessert. She sits silently, pale as a schoolgirl.

"You shouldn't have ordered it all," he says.

She reaches up and removes the little earrings hooked through the lobes of her ears, as if preparing for bed.

"I knew you wouldn't eat it," he says.

Afterwards they walk around town for a bit. Everything is quiet. She seems withdrawn. Near the cathedral she lags, moving very slowly.

"What's wrong?"

Her voice is quite weak.

"Rien."

He waits for her.

"Do you feel sick?" he insists.

She seems close to tears. She shakes her head reluctantly and standing there, suddenly, beside the looming nave, vomits up the whole meal at her feet, frogs' legs and oysters splashing onto the stones. She retches and gasps for air. Dean steadies her. He glances around and is relieved to find no one watching.

"How do you feel? Do you want to sit down?"

She merely breathes in exhaustion.

"Ton mouchoir," she asks feebly.

He produces it. She holds it to her mouth and then wipes the corners. She tries to smile. She is worried about her shoes. They are perhaps stained. She leans against him and lifts her feet, one after the other, to see.

"They're all right," he tells her. "Would you like some tea?"

"Non. Merci."

"I think it'd be good for you."

"Non," she breathes.

She is ashamed, but purified as well. Her whitened face has lost its harshness and clinging to his arm she follows, chastened, along the dark streets.

The next morning she is recovered. His prick is hard. She takes it in her hand. They always sleep naked. Their flesh is innocent and warm. In the end she is arranged across the pillows, a ritual she accepts without a word. It is half an hour before they fall apart, spent, and call for breakfast. She eats both her rolls and one of his.

In the afternoon they see a Laurel and Hardy movie, a relic of thirty years before. The theatre is a closet. The seats are like torn magazines. Later they walk along the river. The water is grey and seems not to be flowing. She

goes down the bank to pick some cattails for her room.
Dean waits on the path. He can see her choosing the ones
to take, filling her arms. What if she becomes pregnant, he
wonders. The clouds are heavy, their bases dark as lead.
The thought has come quietly, but it embeds itself in him.
He dares not say it aloud. Suddenly he is certain he
doesn't want to marry her. Still, if she were to have a
baby, what could he do? He couldn't simply leave. His
feet are cold. His cheeks feel dry. The chill of the afternoon seems to have entered his soul. She is walking along
down at the water's edge. Dean follows above, slowly,
wondering how it can end.

17

N ow, in the white afternoon, past the bare trees of
the avenue, the car glints along. There is almost
no traffic. The town seems abandoned. He turns
down Boulevard Mazagran, turns again, and then stops,
parking carelessly, at a slight angle to the wall, outside
the Jobs'.

Dean has begun tutoring three times a week. It came
about rather unexpectedly, although the idea must have
been flickering in Madame Job's mind for some time.
When she asked me about it, what my opinion would be,
I was taken by surprise. I had no chance to adjust myself.

"A tutor?" I said. "Of what?"

"But English, naturally."

"Well," I said, "I don't know. I suppose if he were
interested he might be able to."

"*Comme il est gentil,*" she pleaded. She was thin as a
ferret.

"You can always try it."

"Do you think?"

"Oh, yes. Why not?"

She tried to hide her pleasure. It annoyed me.

He is completely the young student for her, brilliant and clean. Her children adore him. He fashions a set of those cards with a picture on one side and the word on the back. His drawings are very clever, of course. The *automobile* is his, the one outside, except even longer and slightly uneven. The chicken looks like Claude Picquet.

His life assumes a nineteenth-century air. He rises at eight or eight-thirty and has coffee. Then he reads the morning paper to strengthen his vocabulary. The headlines are underscored these days, the front pages filled with fragments of that terrible divorce, Algeria, which is in its final agony. Many French still cling to the possibility of triumph, the dominance of will. *La guerre est la domaine de la force morale.* They are like widows, dispossessed tenants, martyrs, maniacs. In the last frenzy, desperate schemes appear. The violence becomes grotesque. Citizens, some with decorations in their lapels, are machine-gunned in the streets. The assassins are practically children. They are sickened by their act. They sit on the curbstone and weep.

In the evenings he's home before midnight. He almost never spends the night with her. Her bed is very small, and then, I think he prefers to be able to leave. Besides, they have the weekends in every old hotel, shutters drawn, door bolted from the inside.

He is elated with his first pay from giving lessons, they go to Avallon. Napoleon has stayed in the hotel there. It breathes of his glory. In the hallways there are prints of the campaigns, Rivoli, Jena, the Mamelukes. The girl at the reception desk has a gold tooth which shines when she smiles.

They sit in the dining room quietly inspecting the

menu, prices first. She has changed upstairs, and beneath her suit she has nothing on. Dean knows this. As he reads, his thoughts keep returning to it. Her body, portions of it, seem to become luminous in his mind. Everything he touches or looks at, the fork, the tablecloth, somehow, by their homeliness, their silence, seem to celebrate that flesh which only a single layer of cloth conceals, does not even conceal, proclaims. She eats a large meal. She even drinks a little wine. Dean gazes at her through his empty glass. A brilliant, irregular world appears. The chandeliers glitter like stars. Her face swims away, crowned in soft hair.

"We make movies tonight," she says.

In confusion he tries to think what that might mean. She sits across the table, smiling at him. Their napkins lie crumpled to the side.

Could she, I have often wondered over the empty plates in restaurants, in cafés where only the waiters remain, by any rearrangement of events, by any accident could she, I dream, have become mine? . . . I look in the mirror. Thinning hair. A face marked by lines, cuts they are, almost, that define my expressions. Strong arms. I'm making all of this up. The eyes of a clever and lazy man, a passionate man . . .

She removes her jacket. Those splendid breasts illuminate the room. She steps out of her skirt, and one hungers for nothing but her, that complaisant her which is so ready to yield. It was by glances, exhausted glances across a nightclub that I discovered her, and I confirmed her only in silence, in stealth, and now all of it is clapped around my consciousness like a ring of iron. Those sovereign breasts, freed of cloth. She loves to be naked. She swims in the light. She is drenched with it.

Great lovers lie in hell, the poet says. Even now, long afterwards, I cannot destroy the images. They remain within me like the yearnings of an addict. I need only hear certain words, see certain gestures, and my thoughts begin to tumble. I despise myself for thinking of her. Even if she were dead, I would feel the same. Her existence blackens my life.

Solitude. One knows instinctively it has benefits that must be more deeply satisfying than those of other conditions, but still it is difficult. And besides, how is one to distinguish between conditions which are valuable, which despite their hatefulness give us strength or impel us to great things and others we would be far better free of? Which are precious and which are not? Why is it so hard to be happy alone? Why is it impossible? Why, whenever I am idle, sometimes even before, in the midst of doing something, do I slowly but inevitably become subject to the power of their acts.

Silence. I listen to it, the silence of that room which leaves me faint. Those calm phrases to which she knows so well how to respond as barefoot now, unhurried, she crosses to him in the dark.

I have not gone deep enough, that's the thing. In solitude one must penetrate, one must endure. The icy beginning is where it is worst. One must pass all that. One must go forward all the way, through bitterness, through righteous feelings, advancing upon it like a holy city, sensing the true joy. I try to summon it to me, to make it appear. I am certain it is there, but it does not come easily. Of course not. One must waver. One must struggle. Beliefs are meant to cleave us to the bone.

"There was a lot," she says.

She glistens with it. The inside of her thighs is wet.

"How long does it take to make again?" she asks.

Dean tries to think. He is remembering biology.

"Two or three days," he guesses.

"Non, non!" she cries. That is not what she meant.

She begins to make him hard again. In a few minutes he rolls her over and puts it in as if the intermission were ended. This time she is wild. The great bed begins creaking. Her breath becomes short. Dean has to brace his hands on the wall. He hooks his knees outside her legs and drives himself deeper.

"Oh," she breathes, "that's the best."

When he comes, it downs them both. They crumble like sand. He returns from the bathroom and picks up the covers from the floor. She has not moved. She lies just where she has fallen.

They always drive somewhere the following day. They rise late and plan a journey. These are the first mild weekends. It's good to be outside. They put their things in the car: her small plastic suitcase, the radio, a copy of *Elle*. She gets in and slams the door.

"Do you have to do that?" he says.

"Sorry."

"One of these times it's going to come right off the damn car."

"I am sorry," she repeats.

"It's all right," he says and really, he is content. Her period started that morning. Everything is fine.

They leave town through a long corridor of trees. The country opens to receive them. Squares of warm sunlight drift across their laps. The rich murmur of the engine flows beneath them. They talk about her friends, Danielle, whose parents own the grocery. And Dominique, who went to live six months with a German family. She liked it very much. Better than France. Anne-Marie would like to go there herself. What about Italy? Oh, yes, of course, Italy. Perhaps they can go to Italy together, she suddenly suggests. In the summer. They could drive.

"Sure," he says. It's all vague and far off.

After a while she begins to move about on the seat.

"Oh, Phillip," she says, "my Tampax is not good. You must stop in Saulieu."

"All right."

"Is it far?"

"Not very," he says.

She gives a faint hiss of dismay. It's really just like her. He admires that. Sometimes she will go into the woods to pee.

18

S lowly the light changes, day by day, reflected from countless old surfaces of the town. A new quality appears in it, an intensity that means death for the season. The winter months have grown weary. They are ready to be overthrown. In the streets one can sense the imminence of this. The skies have grown bright, have freshened. The past is melting like ice.

Dean sits waiting while she makes herself up. It's still fairly light outside. People are strolling after work, happy to have days that end before darkness. He looks through a cheap magazine while she makes the last touches. Her face is close to the mirror.

"You know, you shouldn't read this junk," he says, leafing through it.

She turns to see. Then she continues with the mirror.

"It's just stories," she says.

"They're terrible. What do you see in them?"

She shrugs. He tosses it aside.

"I should read more books," she says, as if to her reflection.

"That's right, you should."

"I like Montherlant," she says. "And Proust."

"You haven't read Proust."

"Of course," she says.

"Really?"

Turning, she asks,

"How do you find me?"

"Too much lipstick," he says.

She turns her head this way and that before the mirror, considering herself.

"I find it good," she says.

"No, it's not."

"*Si,*" she insists. Nevertheless she wipes a little from the corners.

Dean sits on the bed, his head leaning back against the wall. He looks around the room. Everything seems ordinary, everything seems poor. Sometimes he is depressed by her imperfections. They should not be important, perhaps, but they often become so real, so ready to take control of her, these plain qualities hidden by the brilliance of a language and life the taste of which he has only just begun to grasp. He waits for her to put on her coat. She avoids his eyes. In silence they descend to the street. He is waiting for her to say something.

"We go to the shops?"

Dean doesn't reply. He merely stares at her.

"Come," she insists.

It's chilly at this hour, the end of the day. Her cheeks are reddened, like an urchin's. The tiny slits in her earlobes seem a mark of low caste. They walk towards the center of town. She has linked her arm in his. He seems not to notice. He has turned into lead.

"*Tu es fâché avec moi?*" she asks.

He shrugs. They walk along cheerlessly. Her face has the helplessness of someone who is no longer believed in.

"Phillip, *tu es fâché?*" she repeats.

"No."

There are only women in the shop, mothers and daughters, wives. The owner moves among the flutter of merchandise. She is waiting on two or three customers at once. She reaches for boxes on various shelves and lays them open on the counter. Dean is uncomfortable. He stands against the wall like a shadow. He has a pose of disinterest, but although they glance at him upon entering, nobody seems to pay him any attention.

"Phillip," she calls.

He looks up for an instant, uncertain. She had gone to the back.

"Phillip," she calls again, *"viens."*

She beckons from one of the booths.

He starts back. One of the shoppers looks up at him. He feels awkward, as if the process of movement had suddenly asserted all its complexity and everything had to be commanded. He walks as if made of wood. The curtain is pulled aside. There in the company of a large mirror she stands, naked to the waist.

"You must help me," she says calmly.

She slips her arms into a brassière and presents her back to him to have it fastened. He does it without a word, with the detachment of a servant, but as he watches her in the mirror regarding herself, turning slightly, then hunching her shoulders together to take it off again, he begins to have an erection.

"You must help me choose," she says. A pause. "Phillip."

"Yes."

"You must help me."

He is watching her. Her nakedness compels him. No matter what he does, he cannot commit it to memory. It seems to be given to him in a series of revelations that are like flashes. She makes her breasts comfortable in another garment which he fastens.

"Do you like it?" she asks.

"I like the other more," he says. His first words. She gives not the slightest hint of triumph.

"This?"

"Yes."

She strips to try it on again.

"Yes," she agrees. "This one is the best."

She raises her arms to allow him to feel it. After a few minutes she removes the brassière and watches in the mirror as his touch makes her nipples hard. Someone begins walking towards the rear of the shop, and Dean starts to move away, but she tightens her arms against her sides to imprison him. They hear the curtain of the other booth being pulled aside for a young girl and her mother. In the mirror Dean discovers a smile.

They go off to dinner near the *gare*. The sky is unnaturally bright. In the last of day a great storm assembles. The air is alive. Across a heaven of terrifying, of Toledo blue, huge clouds are moving, dark as the sea. People begin to vanish. The open spaces of town, the promenades, the squares, become thrilling in their emptiness. A cat hesitates, then hurries across the street.

They eat with the rain coming straight down, smoking across the pavements. Dean is excited. His whole mood has changed. Great bands of water move through the darkened air and beat on the cloth of his car.

"Isn't that beautiful?" he cries.

He is hunched over the table, looking out.

"*Tiens*," she says, "are you happy now, seal? There is water."

He nods, ashamed of how he has been, which seems childish. The storm is the first of spring. It turns one's thoughts ahead. Her freckles—she does not know the word—will come back, she says. Not everywhere, just here, she circles her eyes and nose.

"Ah," he says. "You'll be like a raccoon."

"A what?"

"A raccoon. A raccoon," he says. "Don't you know what that is? It's an animal."

"Oh, yes?" she says blankly.

Suddenly he bursts into laughter. He cannot contain it. He tries to tell her: *c'est très joli,* but he can't say it, and she begins laughing, too. He starts to draw one for her on a scrap of paper. First the feet, but they are absurd. He collapses in laughter.

"It's a rat," she says.

"No, it's not."

However, he cannot keep it from becoming that. Its ears. Even its tail. The nose grows very pointed.

"It's a rat," she says.

They need only glance at each other to start laughing again.

In the room she tries on her new things. She slips off her clothes and puts on the pants and bra she's just bought. Then she poses for him, laughs, and falls onto the bed. They lie together in the calm darkness. He places her hand on his prick. Her cool fingers hesitate a moment and then begin to comprehend it. She is more obedient than before. He is more devoted. The bath of anger has left them happier. It's like a pruning. Afterwards they seem less encumbered—they move towards the very light.

A long time passes. Her head rests on his chest. She begins to kiss his stomach. The gravity of her movement betrays her. Suddenly he is certain of what she is about to do. He draws her up and presses kisses on her mouth. He can already feel it fitting over him. She moves down again. Her body is curled between his legs. Tenderly she explores him. Finally she begins. Dean touches her cheeks. He traces his finger around her mouth, outlining it. She stops as if for breath, then starts again, accepting more of it. He thrusts a little. He feels himself come. Great, clenching bursts. She doesn't move. She draws back slightly. Finally she relinquishes him altogether. A solemn moment somehow occurs. She spreads part of the sperm on his belly with her index finger while she watches the last, reflexive spasms. Then she goes to the sink. Dean hears the water running. Was it bad, he asks. She spits out some water and says something in French. He doesn't understand.

"What?"

She is silent.

"What is it like?" he asks.

She returns to the bed. She doesn't know. Strange, is all she will say. Strong. It's her first time.

19

One afternoon visiting the source of the Marne, or perhaps it's at Azay-le-Rideau, nothing is certain, they stroll in the mild sunlight and talk of the ways to love, the sweet variety.

"What are they?" she wants to know.

Dean begins casually, arranging as he does a bouquet of alternatives to conceal the one he really desires. He has said it a hundred times to himself, rehearsing, but still his heart skips. She listens impassively. They walk slowly, looking at the ground. They seem, from afar, like school-mates discussing, perhaps, an exam.

"It must hurt," she says.

"No," he says. Then, very naturally, "if it does, we stop.

"We can try it," he adds.

There is no reply, but she seems to agree. Yes. Some-

time. He feels a moment of dizziness, as if he has run
from a theft. He begins to explain it further, to fashion a
derivation, to make it rare, common, whatever seems
right. She understands only a little of what he is saying.
Dean is talking deliriously. Finally he recognizes it and
forces himself to stop. They have come to the car. He
opens the door for her and then walks around to the
driver's side. He gets in himself, becomes busy with the
keys. Why, she asks, has he waited so long to tell her
about this. He cannot think of what to answer.

"I don't know," he says. "All in good time."

"*Comment?*"

She's very matter of fact. He shakes his head—nothing. She looks at him, and he feels nervous. She has
thrown him into despair.

Then, in that great car that exists for me in dreams,
like the Flying Dutchman, like Roland's horn, that ghosts
along the empty roads of France, its headlights faded, its
elegance a little shabby; in that blue Delage with doors
that open backwards, knees touching, deep in the seats
they drive towards home. The villages are fading, the rivers turning dark. She undoes his clothing and brings forth
his prick, erect, pale as a heron in the dusk, both of them
looking ahead at the road like any couple. Her fingers
form a ring which she gently slips onto it and then causes,
cool, to descend. Her slim fingers. She turns to see what
she is doing. Dean sits like a chauffeur. He is barely
breathing.

"I like your *profil*," she says. "How do you say that?"

"Profile." His voice seems lost.

"I like your profile. No, I *love* your profile. Like is
nothing."

She is in a good mood. She is very playful. As they
enter her building she becomes the secretary. They are
going to dictate some letters. Oh, yes? She lives alone, she

admits, turning on the stairs. Is that so, the boss says. *Oui.*
In the room they undress independently, like Russians
sharing a train compartment. Then they turn face to face.

"Ah," she murmurs.

"What?"

"It's a big *machine à écrire.*"

She is so wet by the time he has the pillows under her
gleaming stomach that he goes right into her in one long,
delicious move. They begin slowly. When he is close to
coming he pulls his prick out and lets it cool. Then he
starts again, guiding it with one hand, feeding it in like
line. She begins to roll her hips, to cry out. It's like minis-
tering to a lunatic. Finally he takes it out again. As he
waits, tranquil, deliberate, his eye keeps falling on lubri-
cants—her face cream, bottles in the *armoire.* They distract
him. Their presence seems frightening, like evidence.
They begin once more and this time do not stop until she
cries out and he feels himself come in long, trembling
runs, the head of his prick touching bone, it seems. They
lie exhausted, side by side, as if just having beached a
great boat.

"It was the best ever," she says finally. "The best."

He is staring upwards in the dark.

"Phillip?"

"Yes," he says.

"What a *machine,* eh?" she says. "Was it always so
good?"

"I don't think so."

She touches him. He is still quite large.

"I think it's bigger," she says.

"A little, perhaps."

"We must type more letters," she says.

The night is not cold. It is quiet, piercingly clear.
Across the dark roofs, crowded close, the spires of town
rise, illuminated, steeped in terrestrial light.

20

These slow days with their misty beginnings, the fields all cool and quiet, the great viaduct still. Everything is white, everything empty, everything except the earth itself which seems to have awakened. There is an odor in the air that means France still lives. As the morning continues, the mist disappears. Slowly now, the shape of things is revealed. Roofs emerge. The tops of trees. Finally the sun.

I am making an extraordinary record of this town. I am discovering it, bringing it to light. There are photographs of the house alone, nothing but that, the surfaces of furniture, the broad doors, reflections in mirrors, that are the most compelling I have ever made. It almost seems the work of a sick man, work of great patience and simplicity. It has a radiance, a tubercular calm. The children playing by the fountains will become old men, but nothing of this will have changed. There are periods when I am certain of that. My work begins to seem huge. I will be able to enclose myself in it, to have people introduce me.

Near the edge of town there are sheep, a large flock, and two black dogs, lean and endlessly circling, that move it along. They seem to be carving the flock. They curve in behind and mould it. I never hear them bark, but the bleats carry faintly across the still air. Near the front, one old ram limps along. The sun is warm now. The sheep move in a current, like a stream—the edges cling, the center continually flows. The pattern is always changing. Segments seem to break away and vanish farther on. Eddies appear. The sheep hesitate and clog. Some lambs have already been born, and they hurry along behind their mothers. Then, quite mysteriously, the entire flock

stops. Slowly it begins to spread. The animals graze out-
wards. The dogs linger. It's at this moment I see the shep-
herd in a dark, tattered coat. He walks along quietly, an
old man who has watched over them since daylight when
the mist hid them all. Probably he has slept in his clothes.
The lambs look very young. They have long legs. They
hurry to keep up with the fat, indifferent ewes.

It's still too early in the year for Claude to go down to
the river and swim before work. She always goes on her
bicycle. She has no car. Perhaps when she is married
again . . . because I have heard she is about to become engaged to a student from Bourges. He's younger than she
is. Some say twenty-two. I visualize him sitting between
the voluptuous mother and that wise, level-eyed child.
Perhaps he doesn't recognize the dangers. Or maybe they
have their own appeal for him. In any case, it's generally
agreed Madame Picquet is very fortunate to have this
suitor. A little shrug after that. It's quite plain how it was
done.

I see things now in a different light. In a way, I'm
quite relieved to hear about it. There's a good reason why
I've never been able to fulfill my longings—she's been in
love with someone else the whole time. He came to visit
practically every weekend. So really, I would have been
unsuccessful anyway. It's comforting to realize that. And
a student, well, one doesn't mind envying a student. It's
much better than a jeweler, say, or the owner of a bar.
Eventually I discover his name: Gerard.

These calm mornings. Anne-Marie crossing the Place
du Carrouge. It's very small. There's a grocery, a little
café, a fish store. She walks to work, her heels echoing on
the pavement like shot, still a bit of warmth from the bed
clinging to her, her flesh warm still and unwary, her
mouth sullen. Dean is still asleep. His clothes are strewn
about. The shutters are closed. He never dreams. He's

like a dead musician, like a spent runner. He hasn't the strength to dream, or rather, his dreams take place while he is awake and they are marvelous for at least one quality: he has the power to prolong them.

Duration is everything. One knows that instinctively. It hangs over the two of them like an unpronounced sentence. It lies in their bed. All of Anne-Marie's joy proceeds from the hope that they are only beginning, that before them is marriage and farewell to Autun, while like the negative from which her dreams are printed, he perceives the opposite. For Dean, every hour is piercing because it is closer to the end. I'm not sure he is conscious of it. Can he really sense his own destiny? Perhaps—I cannot tell.

Tuesday night. A sandwich at the Foy. Dean's throat is sore, and she has a little cough. She's tired. It's been a difficult day, and she wants to go to bed early.

"Good," he agrees.

"But not alone."

"I'm tired, too."

"No."

"Come on," he says. "We'll see."

"No!" she insists.

They walk through the long, melancholy passage off rue de la Terrasse. On the ground floor are little shops, apartments above. There's a glass roof with laundry hanging beneath it. In daylight one can see the sky. It's like a ruined *palazzo.* Their shoes scuff on the tiles. Through the far end, the trees of the *place* can be seen.

He is chilly and feels weak. He lies in the bed hugging himself and trying to get warm as he watches her undress. Her small navel appears, a bead of a navel and a belly flat and smacking as a flounder. She glances at herself in the mirror, over her shoulder. She likes her behind. It's not shaped like a drop of oil, she says, which one sees all the time, but rather like two *pommes.* Dean is indifferent.

"I don't have anything," he warns as she slips in beside him.

"You don't need it."

"It's safe?"

"*Oui,*" she says. "*Huit jours avant, huit jours après.*"

He is silent. The formula is from her mother. He
counts to himself.

"It's over eight days."

"No."

"Yes, it is," he says.

"No."

Mechanical love. Senseless love. She is dry, and that
makes it worse. Afterwards she tells him she knew exactly how it would be. First he says that he doesn't feel
well. Dean listens unhappily. Then, she says, he suggests
they go home, but not together. Finally he wants to know
whether it's safe or not.

"I know you perfectly," she says.

"Do you?"

"Perfectly. Yes."

He doesn't answer. He recognizes himself.

"Poor Phillip, I want to hurt you."

"You're not hurting me," he says.

"Yes. I want to."

He is watching her in the dark.

"I want you to remember," she says.

He says nothing.

"Could you ever imagine me not?"

"*Pardon?*"

"Do you think I won't?"

She shrugs.

There is an interlude. They lie near each other like
two sick children, exhausted. The last light has gone.
After a while she sits up and puts on her panties. Then
she unlocks the door. The light from the hall shows her
clearly.

"Hey," Dean says, "what are you doing? You can't go like that."

"Nobody is here," she says.

"Put something on."

She looks down at herself for a moment.

"There are people next door," he says.

"Nobody sees."

She slips out as she is, barefoot, her breasts bare.

"Come here!" he whispers. "Put something on!"

He can hear her enter the malodorous little compartment at the end of the hallway and afterwards, faintly, her cough. When she comes back, she slips off her panties again before getting into bed.

"I'm cold," she says.

Her feet are dirty, he thinks.

"Is it true the women in the United States have something to keep them safe all month long?" she asks.

"Sure."

"They don't have it in France," she says. She is caressing him.

"They have a number of things."

"I love it when it's soft and small," she says. She feels his thighs. "I love your body."

Her hand returns to his prick which is swelling with blood.

"*Allo*," she says.

Far off the trains are switching and being assembled. The cars come together with great, metal claps.

"I believe I know him better than you do," she says.

"Yes?"

"I have felt him more."

"Have you ever thought of going to America?" Dean asks. He is working his prick into her slowly.

Silence.

"Annie . . ."

"Yes."

"Have you?"

"Yes," she admits. "Sometimes . . ."

They begin an Olympian act as the freights slam together in the distance. She leaves herself completely. She
moves and cries out like a woman of forty with her lover
for the last time. Afterwards she lies strewn across him.

"You are bread and salt," he tells her.

"Oh, Phillip," she says. They are lost in the darkness.
"*Oui . . .*"

She does not continue. Finally, in a soft voice,

"You are good for me."

The last bells are sounding. The pigeons sleep. In a
moonlight like milk, beneath the worn façades, the Delage is parked close to a few Renaults and an old, boxlike
Citroen. Yes, Dean thinks, America. They will live in a
studio downtown with a small garden, a terrace perhaps,
and a few good friends.

21

Pale end of day and the station empty. In the cafés
the lights are not yet on. Dean sits outside at one of
the iron tables. Along the tree-lined street which
comes down from the square, small, almost alone, Anne-
Marie descends. She turns the corner. One can almost
hear her footsteps. The pigeons hurry away from her, uncertain where to go, cross back, flutter and finally burst
upwards on creaking wings. When they are gone the
quiet returns, the quiet of a hospital.

It is curious how I have begun to discern patterns,
motifs that somehow had no significance for me at the
time. As I view once more the many fragments of this encounter, as I touch them, turn them around, I find myself

subject to sudden, illuminated moments. Meeting at the station, for instance. I had never really considered that. But then I remember that Dean, having left college the first time, spent six months in travel, driving to Mexico and then on to California, the legendary coast. And I think of the very symbol of his existence which continually appears and reappears to me, emerging from behind the trees in the dusk, its lights floating out, its dark shape fleeing along the road, that great, spectral car which haunts the villages, its tires worn, the chrome on its wheels beginning to speckle with rust. Journeys and intimations of journeys—I see now that he has always kept himself close to the life that flows, is transient, borne away. And I see his whole appearance differently. He is joined to the brevity of things. He has apprehended at least one great law.

She comes along the sidewalk to join him, a cheap, metallic blouse over her slacks. She looks like a tramp. Dean adores her. She says something as she sits down, a vanished word, and he nods. And now the waiter appears in a soiled, white coat.

Around the Champ de Mars a green Oldsmobile is turning, black soldiers inside. They are wearing sunglasses. My blood jumps. I can see them as they go by, very slowly, not talking, taking it all in. They are going to recognize me, suddenly I'm certain of it. I can't look at them. The negro lover who has been seeking her for months has finally arrived. The car is going to stop across the street from the café and three men step out, lazily slamming the doors. The fourth remains in the back seat. My mind is racing. Is it him? Is he the one to whom she will be delivered? Dean is pushing someone. There's a scuffle among the chairs.

Of course, it never happens. I have invented it all, their vengeance, their slow, deliberate walk. Instead, they drive slowly around the square, turning, turning. I become calm as I see them stop near the direction signs, read, and then head off on the road to Dijon.

The darkness has come down, and they walk in its fragrance. They reach her street. In the fruit store the lights are still on. The Corsicans are drinking. They're in their undershirts, passing a bottle of wine back and forth as they sit half-buried among the crates. The floor is covered with newspapers. One can hear them laughing. A cat slips out the door.

"They're very nice," Anne-Marie says. "I pass them on the stairs. They always stand aside."

They're all sons, dark, the short hair curling out of their shirts.

"I find them good-looking," she says.

She opens the door to her room. The key rattles. Dean is nervous. In his clothing he conceals, like an assassin, a small tube of lubricant—he would be frightened to have it seen. Still, it exists, cool as a surgical instrument. His answers are vague.

"I love the smell of the fruit," she says.

She has opened the shutters. The room is darker than the night outside. Dean stands close behind her. She is quite naked. Air as cool as water washes over them.

"Can you smell it?" she asks.

"Yes."

They lie in bed. The minutes seem somehow suspended. He feels she is waiting. He is afraid to recognize the moment.

"Do you want it that way?" he says. His voice sounds unfinished.

She was expecting it. She hesitates.

"Ne me fait pas mal."

She watches in silence as he lays a thin coating on his prick. The strength seems to have left her. She behaves as if she has been condemned. He lowers himself carefully onto her back. He is determined to perform the most gentle act, but he doesn't know exactly where to enter. He tries to find it.

"Plus haut," she whispers.

His arms are trembling. Suddenly he feels her flesh give way and then, deliciously, the muscle close about him. He tries not to press against anything, to go in straight. She is breathing quickly, and as he withdraws on the first stroke he can feel her jerking with pleasure. It's the short movements she likes. She thrusts herself against him. Moans escape her. Dean comes—it's like a hemorrhage—and afterwards she clasps him tightly. He can feel faint annular twitches. He lies perfectly still until these final agonies, these quenching hugs which draw the last semen from him, subside. Then he withdraws. There is a tight, failing embrace of the head, then that, too, is gone. They have parted.

"Did you like it?" he asks.

"Beaucoup."

22

A feast of love is beginning. Everything that has gone before is only a sort of introduction. Now they are lovers. The first, wild courses are ended. They have founded their domain. A satanic happiness follows.

They are off to Besançon on the weekend, filled with feathers, floating in pure joy. The spring road flies beneath them. She likes to talk about it. Tell me what you want, she says. I want to please you.

"I like it when you do," he says.

"No," she insists, "tell me."

They walk in the park, submerged in a coolness like old walls. The benches are empty. They are alone. At this hour of evening the sun is gone. The sky, as if summoning itself for the last time, is a piercing, a pale blue, so clear it frightens. It seems that every sound has fled. They walk without speaking, hip against hip. He feels an utter, a complete happiness. The dark fragrance of the trees washes down on them. Their shoes are dusty. The last light fails.

In the dining room they sit across the table from each other. The hotel is spacious and in need of small repairs. Dean is filled with a sense of certainty. It's all familiar. He feels he has been here many times before. This is a returning. If he asks her to go upstairs after the soup, she will put her napkin on the table without hesitation. His eyes examine her face. She smiles.

The owners of the hotel, she points out, are probably *pieds-noirs*, Algerians. Dean looks around. The two young men behind the cashier's desk are very dark. Maybe *juifs*, she adds.

"They don't look it."

"You can tell," she says.

In the room she seems thoughtful. She takes her things off slowly.

"How is it that you are not married?" she asks.

Dean is protean. He is aware of his muscles, his teeth. Life seems to have saturated him, and yet he feels quite calm.

"Go slow," she says.

"*Oui.*"

His devotion is complete; he is beginning to sense the confusion that arises from the first fears of what life would be like without her. He knows there can be such a thing, but like the answer to a difficult problem, he cannot imagine it.

There are many days now when he is perfectly willing to accept the life she illustrates, to abandon the rest.
Simple, vagrant days. His clothes need pressing. There
are fleabites on his ankles.

"No," she says. "Not fleas."

"Listen, I know what they are."

"There are no fleas in French hotels," she says.

"Of course not."

They stroll along the streets, pausing at shoe stores.
He allows her to walk on a bit without him. She stops and
turns. They stand this way, twenty feet apart. Then,
slowly, he comes to her. They walk hand in hand. Her
mother has invited them to lunch the first of April. Dean
nods. It doesn't alarm him.

"We can go?" she says.

"Yes, of course."

"She wants to meet you."

"Fine."

He likes to start into her sometimes while she is talking. She falls still, the words floating down like scraps of
paper. He is able to make her silent, to form her very
breath. In the great, secret provinces where she then exists, stars are falling like confetti, the skies turn white. I
see them in the near-darkness. Their faces are close. Her
mouth is pale and tender, her lips unrouged. Her open
body radiates a warmth one must be quite close to feel.
They are discussing the visit to St. Léger. She describes it
all. It's very pleasant to arrange the day, the hour they
will go, who they are likely to encounter. She talks about
her parents, the house, the woman next door who always
asks about her, the boys she used to go with. One has a
Peugeot now, that's not bad, eh? One has a Citroen. Her
mother tells her about all the accidents—that's what worries her most. Dean listens as if she were unfolding a marvelous story full of invention, a story which, if he wearies
of it, he can suspend with the simplest of gestures.

A splendid noon, the sky flooded with light. They drive along the canal. St. Léger seems quiet and the house itself, as they approach it, empty. Anne-Marie jumps out. She's seen her cat. She picks it up and carries it in her arms.

The meal is served in the kitchen. It begins with a kind of cheese pie. They watch to see if Dean will like it. It's very chill in the room even though the day is warm. Perhaps it's the tile floor, he thinks, or the walls—he isn't sure. He nods at the conversation which he only half understands. His flesh feels blue. Suddenly he realizes he must be getting sick, but then her mother rises to get a scarf. As she sits down again she remarks that it's a little cold. The father shrugs. Dean has been unable to exchange a word with him. They sit like strangers. It is Anne-Marie who talks, mostly to her mother and quite gaily, as if only the two of them were there. Occasionally she asks Dean if he understands. He tells her yes. The father sits like an Arab. He has a lean face. A long nose. He's wearing a cap. He looks at the table or out the window. At one point his wife reaches over to pat his hand. He appears not to notice.

Dean feels increasingly nervous. He is sitting all alone. He doesn't like to look at the father whose eyes are pale and watery, a convict blue. As for the talk, it washes across him like water. He no longer even hears familiar words.

"Phillip, did you understand?" she says.

"*Oui,*" he replies sleepily.

"*Oui?*" the mother asks, her bright gaze on him. For a moment he is afraid they are going to question him.

"*Quelquefois,*" Anne-Marie says, "*il comprend très bien.*"

The mother laughs. Dean lowers his head. He feels the unhurried gaze of the father on him. He tries to return it, is determined to, but involuntarily his eyes flicker away for an instant, and that is enough. It's finished. He knows he has been measured. In revenge he begins to think of their daughter naked, images as unforgivable as slaps. The father lights a cigarette.

He tries once more to concentrate on what they are saying, but it's all too fast. He hardly understands a word. Everything seems to have left him. He begins to count his forkfuls, then the wall tiles.

After lunch he is shown through the house. It's clean and bare. Her room is upstairs, plain as a cell. Somehow he cannot associate all of this with her, it's more like a school she has attended. He looks out of her window. Below, parked in the sunlight, is a long convertible, the seats of real leather. The whole town has seen it.

Her father hasn't left the kitchen. He sits with the newspaper in a chair moved back against the wall and smokes a thick, workman's cigarette, barely inhaling. When they come downstairs it's as if he doesn't hear them. He continues reading as they enter the room.

Dean is depressed and also angry. She tells him not to pay any attention, her stepfather is stupid. It doesn't matter, everything has lengthened the day, made it desolate. The table is right beside the stove. The plates were set on it bare. Her mother made her drink a glass of milk. Somehow the afternoon has turned into their repossession of her, nor has she struggled at all to resist it. She has deserted him. The past has reclaimed her.

"My mother needs a television," she comments as they drive. "All the others have one. It's very lonely at night. She could look."

"I guess so," he says.

"Now she has nothing. It would be very nice, don't you think?"

"Yes," Dean says.

"She needs an automobile, too. A Renault. She bicycles into town, but she is too old for that. Every day. I must get her a Renault."

"Why don't you get her a Mercedes?" Dean says acidly.

"It's too big."

They come to a long, straight section of road, and he begins to accelerate. He seems absorbed in it. They go faster and faster. The gauge finally touches a hundred and sixty. Anne-Marie says nothing. She sits looking out the side.

I meet them for dinner in a restaurant near the square. It's the weekend, a few people more than usual. Still, it's far from being crowded. There's a zinc bar, I think the only one in town. The waitress leans against it and waits to pick up dishes from the kitchen. Dean is drinking *vin blanc*. He's very talkative. I sit there listening to his description of European life, drawing it forth by silence. Of course, he is speaking a special language, rich with deceptions. I brush away tobacco crumbs on the bar, nod, yes, agree. He is telling me about cheeses, architecture, the genuine, the profound intelligence of this civilization. Occasionally there are brief glimpses of cities, certain small hotels.

Anne-Marie sits quietly and as Dean talks, becoming drunker, his mouth wetting, I try to watch her, to isolate elements of that stunning sexuality, but it's like memorizing the reflections of a diamond. The slightest movement and an entirely different brilliance appears. Of course, it is her face I am searching, her gestures, expression. I am interested in the visible. I know quite well what is the source of all her power, but I am trying to identify it by the most commonplace details.

In the pictures I have, she appears strangely grave,

the Saturday when we all shopped in the open market. There are some of her sitting in the car, and some, too, in which there is a faint trace of gaiety, the kind reserved for companions one is loyal to forever. She liked to pose. I gave her prints, of course. She was very pleased. She sent them to her mother, Dean told me.

They are like a couple who've had an argument. As we talk, Dean's eyes keep going past me to the waitress who is speaking, just a few words at a time, to the barman, and who, in between, gives little sighs of resignation.

"I'm nice than she is," Anne-Marie says.

"Nicer than who?"

"Her."

"Certainly you are."

"She looks very well with her clothes," Anne-Marie says, "but how does she look naked? What a shock that must be."

"Shock?"

"Shock?" she repeats. "That's right?"

"Yes, that's good. That's a new word for you."

She shrugs.

"Where did you learn that?"

She makes a vague gesture.

"Well, you're right," he says, "it would probably be shocking. Do you think she makes love?"

A dry laugh. "Of course."

I'm afraid to turn around. Perhaps she even understands what we're saying.

"You're sure?" Dean says.

"My God!"

"OK."

"Look at her eyes," Anne-Marie says. "There are dark rings under them."

"So?"

"That's a sure sign."

That amuses Dean. He begins looking around the room.

"How about that girl sitting by the window?"

"Which one?" she says.

It's early when we leave, not yet ten. We walk along together for a way and then, at a corner, part. I can follow them without thinking. I know how they will go, which shops they will pause in front of, how they will cut across the shamble of tiny streets. They are passing the photographer's, the window Dean loves with its prints of wedding couples, its graduation classes. There is a certain ageless quality to the photos, a redolence of 1914, 1939. They are like old newspapers. Perhaps the shop has been here all that time. Still, there is not one face that could be Dean's. I look carefully along the rows, even at those partly hidden. He will never be found among them. His face emanates a complete, almost a bitter intelligence that doesn't exist here. When I look at his photos, the one that was taken eating an orange, glancing up, on that November day we first went to Beaune—looking at it I see the eyes of Lorca, of someone who is to be taken out of life and destroyed, we will never find the reason. I sit and stare at this picture which is vivid with its own instant, this photo taken before the war, before the revolution. We stopped beneath the viaduct that day. He knew no one. He was going to be here for a week or two, not more.

24

P rangey. The village is poor. As they turn off the road, chickens scatter before them, and then a course of trees appears to indicate the way. They cross a little bridge and drive in, beneath the towers. A dark entry to a white court. On the far side, the huge country house where they will stay, a piece in the stone necklace that is strung across all of France, the piers upon which her history is founded. They have opened their doors to travelers, these *châteaux*. They have become hotels. The great rooms, eloquent in their calm, may be taken by anyone, rooms that have seen the light and darkness of centuries. People can now walk around them in underclothes, lie in the beds like drunken servants.

The door closes. They are alone. It's a vast room with many mirrors. Anne-Marie looks in the bath. Enormous too, and beneath its windows a moat filled with frogs. She takes off her shoes. The carpeting is blue. No sound but the countryside. Birds. The hum of spring. On the wide bed they are soon at work, skillfully, silent as thieves. They are deep in a sumptuous dream in which they have discovered one another.

The sky is pale and drained of heat. In this silence like folded flags, Dean's awareness of things seems extraordinary. He puts his prick into her slowly, guiding it with his hand. It sinks like an iron bar into water. Her eyes close. Her voice is cut adrift.

Minutes. The gravel of the court whispers. Raising up a little, Dean is able to see out the window which is partly open. There are voices. A large family has returned from walking in the gardens and now, amid laughter, begins to arrange itself at the tables while the waiter, in a white coat and black trousers, serves them. The women want Perrier. The men take wine. They are just below—the nearest ones can't be seen. The talk, only a bit dissevered, rises up as if to include him. He withdraws somewhat to watch, taut, supported by his arms, just the tip of his prick inside her. He looks down along his belly to affirm it.

They fuck in lovers' sunshine, in the midst of the party. Her flesh gleams like fabric, intermixed with glimpses of women in silk dresses grouped around the table, children, a friendly dog. The noon hours are drifting away. The waiter brings more ice. It seems to last for hours. They are united by a bloodstream which carries the same sensations. He is nourishing her, touching her heart. When he comes, it's as if a marvelous deception has ended. Afterwards she kisses his prick. His balls. The people have gone. The waiter is alone in the court below, collecting the glasses.

That night they dance in Dijon, in the *boîte* where we saw her first. It's her idea. I'm a little surprised by that. I cannot rid myself of the feeling that she would prefer not to encounter the past, but she seems not to mind. It means nothing to her. The sweat shines on their faces as they move. The armpits of her dress are stained. They drive back at midnight with the top down. It's cool. The roads are empty. The great, worn front of the house is dark, and they park on the expiring gravel. Legs weary, they climb the stairs.

Dean is looking at himself in the mirror while she undresses. He is naked. He stands full on, his hands at his sides. He sees himself as a different person. He is delighted with his thinness, with his hair which is too long, and with the triumphant reflection of himself. He is aware of her moving about behind him, but it is his own nudity he is interested in, a nudity which the glimpses of her presence make thrilling. He discovers himself in her presence, that's the thing. It is the reflection all others must play against. He is pleased with himself. His prick seems murderously large.

"How do we make love tonight?" she asks.

She waits. She is able to summon up all of the black countryside that surrounds them, silences in which every object, every form is at rest. The invisible leaves—the night is filled with them—brush one another lightly. The grasses are still. If one listens closely: the trickle of water below the windows, down a face of rock and into the green scum. The sound of a frog. In the heart of this, in a tall room with its curtains drawn against morning they lie, the faint acid of sweat dried on them and other wetness as well, clear, caking. They were too tired to rise afterwards. They sleep without moving, the blanket drawn over them against the chill of dawn.

25

*T*he relics of love: the title of a page in his notebook. Many entries make no sense. There's a code, of course. Every diarist invents one. *When I die*, he writes, *I would like it to be in a city like Nancy.*

Under *Ideas* he has:

1. When to leave.
2. One meal at a time.
3. Three immortal things: virtue, words, deeds.

And there is a long list of towns, some with a star (Bourges, Montargis). After Malène is written: *long summer*. Names of many cheeses.

The relics of love. His phrases appear spontaneously among mine. Of course I am aware of it, but one must know when to appropriate. He doesn't need them, and for me they are essential. Walls—I mean foundations—would literally crumble without them. For the want of them, entire structures might disappear.

They considered many summer towns. Eze and La Baule. Le Zoute. Arcachon. Finally they decide to drive the Loire. A hot afternoon. It is not yet dark. In the cool of her room they lie like fish in the shadows of a bank. Dean unfolds the map. The shutters are drawn. Some workmen are fixing the rain gutters outside. The sound of their tools, their casual voices close by, is alarming, as if they might suddenly open the room like a tin can and discover the occupants. Dean is completely dressed, but she is almost naked. Her flesh seems polished. The pale nipples look soft as *fraises des bois.*

Yes, the Loire. They are talking in whispers. He smooths out a crease in the map. The great *châteaux* loom blue as peaks along the silent river. They will go in May, late in the month. Chambord rises from its forest. Chenonceaux is a bridge of sun-filled rooms. One looks down from the iron balconies of Amboise a thousand feet above the town, balconies from which the Protestants were hung. They will drive to Angers and then on to the sea.

"I think he must love me," Anne-Marie tells her mother.

They are alone in the kitchen. The mother is not sure. Perhaps. Perhaps not.

"*Si,*" her daughter insists.

"Perhaps."

It's irritating to Anne-Marie. She's very proud. To the mother it is unsettling. One should not believe too strongly in a life which can easily vanish. There are many things to fear, things her daughter may tell her about if she remains patient, if she is wise enough not to ask.

"Well, I think he may love you . . ."

"*Oui,*" Anne-Marie insists.

". . . but will there be any reason left for him to want to marry you?"

Anne-Marie shrugs.

"There are reasons," she finally says without conviction.

"He doesn't work . . ."

"So . . . his father is rich."

"That's not the same."

"Then it's not the same," Anne-Marie says, impatient.

Her mother reaches across to touch her hand, but she has risen and is looking at herself in the mirror. There she finds all she needs. She turns her face a little this way, then that. The sea will appear before them, washed in sunlight. They will walk along the rocks. The white birds rise up lazily as they approach. All the hotels of the coast beckon with their white façades, plum, oyster, dove blue.

Chambord, built by François I, a great, bearded king with eyes small as a boar's. He loved to hunt. He went there with his mistresses and walked up and down in the firelit rooms with his long hair, his rich, dark beard . . . Dean puts a circle around it. The workmen have gone. The sky is a last, clear blue. The air is calm. It's the hour for dinner. Tables are set. In the restaurants the waiters stand quietly near the bar. The monuments, the buildings disappear. There is not long to wait before the first, solitary star.

They descend into evening. The small alleys are darkening now. Old women appear in the entrances in their shapeless, black dress. Cats move along close to the wall, pause, and then hurry off as Dean closes the car door. The full voice of the engine. Through a twilight as calm, as enormous as a night at sea, they pass. The villages are still. The buildings are anchored like ships.

In a café she happens to meet a boy who knew her. He is amazed. You've changed a hundred per cent, he tells her. She smiles. Afterwards Dean asks,

"Who was that?"

The brother of a girl she knew. Dean is looking towards the door as if he might return. It annoys him.

The evening is warm. The place reminds her of the one where, all that summer, she went to dance. They must go there sometime, she says. There were two waiters who liked her. One was Italian. The other was very young and sent her flowers, but he was shy. She never went out with him. She never even thought of him until now, this evening, by chance. It was the Italian with whom she spent those noisy hours, who had her for the first time. But the young waiter, how well I know him. He saves his money. His clothes are neat. He walks quietly through town, his eyes lowered. Sometimes at night he stands in the crowd. He sees her smile and his heart falls out of him. Among the dancers turning in the orange light his eyes can find her in an instant. He knows her calves, the shape of her body better than her lover, and those high-heeled shoes with their thin straps, as they move around the floor they are ripping his dreams.

The theatre is half empty. It's a white building cold as a meat plant. Inside, the ceiling is blue, the walls are hung with pleated cloth, like a skirt. The floor is tilted backwards. Everybody sits in back, staring at advertisements on the drop that covers the screen. Suddenly, having come down the aisle, a man mounts the stage. He has a small beard, like Lincoln. His voice is alarming and clear.

"Ladies and gentlemen," he begins. "It's with great pleasure that we are able to present to you tonight one of the most remarkable women in Europe. She is able—I promise this without exception or hesitation—to read the mind of anyone in this room, to describe them without seeing them, to answer questions she cannot hear, to re-

veal secret longings. Don't be afraid. There is nothing embarrassing, nothing unnecessary. It is a demonstration of
a unique mental power, a communication known to the
Hindus, to the peoples of the East. I present to you: Yolande!"

He summons her. She comes up on the stage and
stands beside him in a black, Spanish hat, a gold dress,
her hair in little ringlets. She bows. The audience is too
stunned to applaud, too cautious. She turns to face the
screen. Her partner walks back to where the first row of
people are sitting. He begins to ask her questions which
she answers with her back turned.

"This person . . ."

"*Monsieur* . . ."

"Is it a man or a woman?"

"A man."

"The color of his hair?"

"Brown."

"His suit . . ."

"Grey."

"His shoes . . ."

"Black."

"*Voilà!*" he says.

He moves on.

"These first three . . ." He leans over and whispers to
them. Their heads are close together. He nods, nods, then
stands erect once more. "Can you give me their names?"

Her voice is curiously mechanical. It's as if she is
reading a list.

"Robert. Gilbert. Jean-Paul."

"Their occupations, please. In order."

"Teacher. Clerk. Mechanic."

"Is that right?" he asks them.

They nod. He takes the wrist of a man behind them.
He holds it up.

"And here . . . ?"

"A watch."

"The make?"

"Intra."

"Is that right?" he asks the man. Yes. A nod. "And now, please, Yolande, the exact time . . ."

"Eleven minutes after nine."

"The seconds?"

"Thirty-five."

He allows the owner to look.

"Voilà!" he cries.

Some applause. It's just the beginning. She reads the serial number on franc notes, identifies objects in people's hands, perceives missing buttons, tells dates of birth, hours. The dialogue is sharp and fast.

"This gentleman . . ."

"Monsieur . . ." she cries.

"Is holding . . ."

"A ticket."

"Yes?"

"A railroad ticket."

"To where?"

"To Châlons!"

"Voilà!"

The audience is whispering. He strides back to the stage, arm extended in triumph, fingers curved. Now Yolande herself turns around. She is prepared, she announces, to answer, individually and privately, all questions.

"Your most secret questions," she says as she coolly straps on a leather belt that has a purse attached. For two francs, she will give a personal response. She begins to circulate, asking only the first name before she selects, with great speed, an envelope from the basket she carries. Her partner walks ahead, encouraging people to concentrate on the question they want answered.

"Can I ask her?" Anne-Marie says.

"Go ahead."

He sorts out his change. She raises her hand. Yolande sees her immediately.

"Mademoiselle . . ."

"Oui."

"Your first name."

"Anne-Marie."

"Born," Yolande says, holding out her arm, indicating one moment, "born . . . in the month of October. Correct?"

Anne-Marie smiles dazedly. She nods.

"Voilà!" the man cries. He moves ahead. "Who else? Raise your hands, please."

It's a pale blue envelope, unsealed. Inside is a single sheet of paper, numbered 7. In the top corner, a constellation. At the bottom, a red star. Some of the phrases are underlined in red. She begins reading it quickly.

"Let me see," he says.

There's no answer to any question. It's printed in a style to look like handwriting.

Your nature, it says, *predisposes you to dream. You are capable of deep feelings . . .* Some words he cannot read . . . *at the moment, you are not very lucky, but don't fall into despair. Your destiny will soon be revealed. Courage! Belief!* Her scent is Iris. Her lucky day Monday. He was wrong—at the very bottom there is a response to her thought: *Your desire will be realized if you open your heart.*

"Is that right?" Dean asks.

"No," she says. "It's printed."

"Let me read it again," he says. "Maybe she gave you mine."

"But how did she know the month I was born?" Anne-Marie says.

"She smelled your scent. Iris."

"What do you mean?" she says.

They drive home at midnight. It's not often they're out so late. Usually their evenings are quite simple. A meal somewhere. A stroll from which they return after dark. The trees above them are rich with silence. From the radio stations of Europe music pours forth faintly in the cheapest rooms. Her portable is on the floor. The dial is illuminated. It glows mysteriously. Luxembourg is on. Geneva. The orchestras of the world beat softly. The muscle in her behind is tight. It feels like a string around the shaft. He pushes in slowly and then, at last, plunges, like the bottom dropping out. Anne-Marie moans, her head buried in her arms. After he was dead I thought often of these moments, of this one. Perhaps it is her moan, her face pressing against the sheet. He can feel her tight around him, like a noose. He closes her legs and lies there contented, looking out the window, feeling the tender spasms.

"*Es-tu contente?*" he asks after a while.

Her voice, her very presence, seems summoned from afar. She answers quietly.

"*Oui.*"

26

"**D**on't you get tired of being down there for months on end?" Cristina says. "God!"

I don't know what to say. They're all looking at me. I'm really not sure. It's not a question of being tired of something. It really can't be compared.

"What on earth do you do there?" Alix says.

"Well, I'm doing some work." A pause. "I'm doing a lot of reading—I know that sounds funny."

"It must be fascinating," she says. "Whatever you're reading."

They laugh.

"What is he really doing?" she asks. "It's all so secretive. It must be something marvelous."

I can't tell whether she means it or not. They've asked her to dinner because of me. I'm uncertain how to take her though. She's beautifully dressed in a blue silk suit, and she seems to be completely unaffected by my presence. At first, in fact, she ignored me, but her attention is worse. Billy asks if I want another drink.

"How long are you here for?" Alix says.

"Just a few days. You don't mean in France? Altogether?"

"Yes, in France."

"I don't know," I tell her. "I've already stayed longer than I expected."

"Um," she says. "You like it then."

I can't answer that. Finally I nod. I say,

"Yes."

She turns to Cristina.

"He's rather nice," she says and then, talking to them, abandons me.

By the time we go to dinner, I am nervously trying to play this game with her. It's exciting to be in her company, but I'm always a little afraid of what she might say next, and this fear causes me to be helpless. She's as tall as I am with a very beautiful complexion, not at all pale. I can't tell how old she is. Twenty-six perhaps. I can't very well ask. When Billy and I go down for the car, he tells me she's been married. This puts me more at ease for some reason.

"She was married to Teddy Leighter," he says.

"Who?"

"Teddy Leighter. Don't you know him?"

"I'm not sure. Who is he?"

"Oh, you know him," Billy says.

"I do?"

"Sure you do," he says. "He played hockey."

Then he says something I don't hear. But we've arrived at the level of the garage.

We have dinner at the Calvados in a room filled with candles. I notice she reads the menu carefully, even with interest, but she practically ignores the food when it arrives. In the middle of the meal she tells me she'd like some Evian water. She goes on talking to Cristina while I try to find a waiter. A night, a long night in which I am captive, is beginning. It will end with a determined search for the negress we saw last time in the club near the Champs. Alix and I have to see her, Billy decides.

"I've seen her."

"But Alix hasn't," he says.

Billy looks like a bullfighter, Alix says. She's jealous of him. He'll always be beautiful. She stares at him very directly, her chin in her hand. No, he says and orders more wine. He even moves like a bullfighter, she says. Cristina seems to think it's funny.

The negress cannot be found. Paris is filled with the fresh smell of trees as we go from place to place. She cannot be found, but finally there is another in a dress made of flowers. The room is crowded. Alix dances very close to me.

"Have you really been down there all winter long?" she says.

"Yes. Why?"

"I've been thinking about it, that's all."

"You're embarrassing me," I say. "It's not that interesting to talk about."

"You like it though."

"Yes."

"You must have fallen in love," she says.

"No." Perhaps there was a slight pause.

"Ahh," she says. "That's it. You have a girl."

She smiles at me for the first time. At last we have found each other.

"That's right, isn't it?" she says.

"No."

"Oh, you're lying."

"I'm not."

"You have a little French girl."

"I'm ashamed of it, but I don't."

"They can be very nice," she says.

"I'm sure."

Back at the table she tells them I've confessed. Carrying on a wild affair, she says.

"It's not that woman across the street?" Cristina says.

"Madame Picquet?"

"Is that right?" Billy says happily.

"No, no. She's getting married."

"I thought she was married," Cristina says.

"She's divorced."

"The town whore," Cristina explains.

"Who's she marrying?" Billy says.

"Oh, some student. I don't know. I've never seen him."

"How about you?" he says.

"It's nothing. Alix invented it."

"Come on."

"No. Really." I feel like an idiot.

Alix is smiling. The show comes on again.

"I don't like this singer as much as the other one," Cristina says.

When we finally come out the sky is still dark, but its authority is gone. The night has passed. We drive back to their house. Billy turns on all the lights. He insists on preparing breakfast. He wanders around the kitchen with a huge pan in his hand. He begins to break a dozen eggs into it.

"How about making the toast?" he says.

I'm not even hungry. He gives me a dish with a big square of butter on it, right out of the refrigerator. It's too hard. When I try to spread it, I tear the toast. He is pouring milk into the eggs, then Worcestershire sauce.

"How do you like them?" he asks me. "Hard or soft?"

"It doesn't matter."

He looks at the color.

"They need more milk," he says.

In the long, richly furnished salon, the women are sitting on the sofa. It's almost light outside. The brightness of the room and the windows paling makes it seem like the end of a long crisis. Their hands are moving. I can hear their palms against their wrists. I sit near them.

"What are you doing?"

"Flipping," Cristina says.

They compare coins. Their attention to the game is solemn, unreal.

"We're flipping for you," she says. A pause. "It's one up."

Neither of them looks at me. They match again and hold their wrists near each other. Cristina breaks into nervous laughter.

"Who won?" I ask.

No answer.

"Three out of five," Alix suddenly says.

"All right."

The coins flicker in the air. Cristina drops hers. It doesn't seem right for me to help her find it. She searches the dark, Oriental rug on which it has disappeared.

"It's by the coffee table," Alix says.

"Where?"

"Just inside the leg."

Cristina's on her hands and knees.

"It's heads," she says.

Billy comes in to announce everything is ready.

"What'd you drop?" he says.

"Hm?"

"Where've you been?" Alix says.

We sit in the dining room in the five o'clock light of a Paris morning. Against the wall is a huge, mahogany buffet. Mirrors which reflect the dawn. The table is large enough for twelve. Billy brings in the platter heaping with eggs that smell alarmingly strong.

"What are these?" Alix says, taking a small portion. "Eggs?"

Billy is sitting at one end of the table. He stares at her. He becomes serious when he drinks. Cristina begins laughing. She can't stop. She laughs as she tries to serve herself, and Alix starts in, too. They laugh insanely; helpless, crying laughter. Eggs have spilled from the serving spoon onto the table, and Cristina tries to pick them up. By now she can't even control her hand. She can't look at Alix. They slowly fall into silence, but the slightest sound from either of them starts it again.

"What's so funny?" Billy says. He hasn't even smiled.

"Nothing." The last syllable explodes. They are laughing so much it hurts.

"Aren't you going to eat any eggs?" he finally says.

"What?" Cristina forms the word cautiously.

"I said aren't you going to eat any eggs?"

She shakes her head slowly, no, then yes.

"They're very interesting," she says.

"Are they? Why?"

"I've never tasted eggs quite like these," she says. She tries to become serious. Alix is laughing.

"Is that so?" he says.

"Did you make them, dear?"

"You're very funny," he says.

She gets up and begins opening drawers in the buffet, looking for napkins. Billy hands me the platter. The eggs are very dark, almost brown. They look curdled.

"I don't think they're bad," he says.

Behind him, Cristina suddenly performs an obscene gesture, one hand in the bend of her white arm. It's so deliberate I can't think. Billy is bent over his plate.

"Keep it up," he warns.

"What's that, sweetheart?" she asks.

"You're going to get it," he says.

As she comes back to the table she begins to sing. Somehow it frightens me. I'm exhausted. I don't know how to smile.

"Aren't you even going to try them?" he says.

"Of course," she says. "I love them."

"There's nothing wrong with them," he says flatly. He eats methodically, watching her. He takes a sip of coffee.

I try the eggs. They taste like salt. Cristina strolls around the table humming as she gives everyone a napkin.

"Alix?" she asks sweetly. "More eggs?"

"Sit down, will you, Cristina?" he says. "Aren't you going to eat?"

"You're beautiful," she says. "I love you."

"Just keep going."

"I *love* the eggs. Some more eggs?" she asks me.

Everything is left on the table, the plates with their uneaten portions, the cups of coffee, the toast. The servants will take care of it all when they get up.

I drive Alix home in a taxi in the bright of morning. It's not very far. The dawn smells cool and pure as we cross the sidewalk. She is very sleepy. She releases me with a word or two, a tired smile. The door closes. The lock sounds like a well-ordered life.

I walk back. In the streets there is an absolute silence, not a car moving, not a person. In the pale sky there are no birds. It's like entering the past. Nothing is altered. Nothing makes a noise. On the corner, in the window of a café they sometimes go to, a cat is sleeping, a huge cat, soft as a dream. I pause there, awake before the city. I think of walking along the river, but my whole body is like dry wood. I turn down the street on which they live, a wide street, blue and empty, empty sidewalks as far as I can see.

27

They are still in bed, windows open to the morning coolness. Her face has no make-up, her skin no shine. She has a cheap look in the morning, young, without resources. And then as I watch, they wake at the same instant, like actors, like the cat in the café which opened its eyes to find me staring through the flat glass. Her breath is bad. My images are repeating themselves— there's nothing I can do. I'm too weary to sleep. They crowd in on me. They come again and again, I cannot struggle free. Besides, there is no place to go, they would follow me into dreams.

"*Bonjour*," she says. She kisses his stiffened prick.

"He never smiles," she says, looking it in the eye.

"Sometimes," Dean murmurs. Her mouth feels warm. I try to find darkness, a void, but they are too luminous, the white sky behind them, their bodies open and fresh. They are too innocent. They're like my own children, and they illustrate an affection which has little rea-

son to, which in fact does not exist except that she—at the
very bottom it is her only real distinction—she knows
how to make things come true. Her mouth moves in long,
sweet reaches. Dean can feel himself beginning to tumble,
to come apart, and I am like a saxophone player in a
marching band, in love with a movie queen. Soft-eyed,
lost, I am tramping wretchedly back and forth at halftime.
My thoughts are flailing. The batons flash in mid-air. The
whole stadium is filled. I am marching, turning, marking
time while she slowly circles the field in a new convertible. I am a clerk in her father's brokerage. I'm the young
waiter who sends bouquets of flowers. I am a foreigner
who answers the telephone wondering who can be calling, and it is the police. I cannot understand at first. They
have to repeat it several times. There is an instant when
my heart turns to lead: an accident. A motor car . . .

There is a rise on the road to Sens and then, suddenly,
on the down side, a hundred meters farther on, the skid
marks, tar-black. The road curves. There is broken glass,
motorcycles, people gathered around the wreck. The ugly
underside of a car is showing, turned up to the sky. The
wheels are motionless. A *gendarme* in white leather gaunt-
lets is waving drivers past. People bend over to look beneath the wreckage. There is no haste. Everyone moves
with deliberation. Only a few children are running, out
on the grass.

"It's a Citroen," Dean says. A motorbike is crushed
beneath it. They pass slowly. Now they can see the feet of
someone laid out near the trees. On the paving are dark
runs of blood.

"They're always in accidents," he says. "I don't understand it."

"They're very fast," she tells him.

"Citroens? They're not so fast."

"Oh, yes."

"How do you know? You don't even drive."

"They always pass us," she says.

I know this road well. It leads to Les Settons, the lake where they go to swim. Anne-Marie stands in the shallow water. She has earrings on and a necklace. She bends her knees to immerse herself and then swims like a cat, her neck stiff, her head up. After a moment she stands up again.

"You must teach me," she says to Dean.

He tries to show her the deadman's float. Breathe out through your mouth, he tells her. No. She doesn't like to wet her hair.

"You have to."

"Why?"

"Come on," he tells her. "You can't learn unless you do."

She shrugs. A little puff of contempt—she doesn't care. Dean stands waist-deep in the water, waiting. She doesn't move. She is sullen as a young thief.

"Take your earrings off," he says gently.

She removes them.

"Now do what I say. Don't be afraid. Put your face in the water."

She doesn't move.

"Do you want to learn or don't you?"

"No," she says.

They put their clothes on behind the car. No one else is around. Near the shore the surface of the water is broken by weeds. The leather seats are hot, and when Dean starts the engine small birds skim out of the bank grass and out across the lake.

They eat in Montsauche in a little *auberge*. Sunday. Everything is hushed. Dean sits looking out at the street. It's a silent meal. Afterwards there is nothing to do. He feels as if he is taking care of a child. He is thinking of

other things. The day seems long. They drive—Dean
takes the top down and they head towards Nevers, the
wind curving in, the sun on their backs. He begins to
grow sleepy. They pull off the road.

They lie down under the trees. Pines. It's very quiet.
The dry cones click in the breeze. The shadow of branches
is laid across their faces. Dean closes his eyes. He is almost asleep.

"Phillipe," he hears her say.

"Yes."

"I would like to make love in the woods sometime."

"You've never done that?"

"No."

"Strange," he says.

"You have?"

He lies, "Yes."

"I have never. Is it nice?"

"Yes," he says. It's the last thing he remembers.

When he wakes, he feels cold. He sits up and rubs his
forearms. His skin is creased from the grass. A few dry
pieces are stuck to him.

They walk aimlessly, Anne-Marie brushing the back
of her skirt a little, down to a stream. There's a small, iron
bridge. They stand in the middle of it. Beneath them the
water moves slowly. In places, clear as reflection, one can
see the bottom. There are fish in the shadows, completely
still. The water flows around them.

"Do you see them?" she says.

Dean is dropping pieces of twig. They meet the surface gently, drift away.

"We could catch them," she says.

The pieces are light. They seem to float down from
his fingers.

"Do you like to fish?" she says.

"No."

"No?"

"It's too cruel," he says.

"They don't feel."

"How do you know?"

"Oh," she says, "they don't."

The fish linger, aligned with the flow. A few drift across the pale flats where the water is clear, pass to a deep menstruum, vanish.

"Why catch them?" Dean says. "They're happy."

"Until they are eaten by a *brochet*," she says.

"Well, that's what I'd be," he says. "A *brochet*. Live in the river."

"They would catch you."

No. He shakes his head.

"Yes. Someone."

"Not me," he says. "No. I'd be a very smart *brochet*."

"All right," she says. "And I will be your *brochette*."

The water is moving very slowly. Dean throws a small stone. The surface dissolves. I will be your *brochette*. It is really a quiet, domestic life they are engaged in. Suddenly he perceives this. The phrase pierces him like wire. She smiles. She begins to grow beautiful once more. It is always mysterious how she can change. By evening, in the Etoile d'Or, he can hardly take his eyes from her. She has fixed her hair and made up her face. She butters a piece of bread for him.

"*Ça va?*" she says.

He nips at her finger. The oestrus of night comes down over him like a hood. He can feel it descending, changing his flesh.

They climb the stairs. She goes first, as always. Her calves flash before him, turning away, rising on the narrow treads. Her key opens the door. Dean's prick begins to stir, and as he doubles the pillow later and she rises on her elbows, his mind is already cut loose and wandering as if he cannot keep himself together. He is thinking of what it will be like without her. He cannot repress it. Like the cough of a sick man, a weakness rises to frighten him, an invisible flaw, and he embraces her with a sudden, dumb intensity. Her back, even the word for it is beautiful, *dos,* lies beneath him, the back she never sees, the smooth intelligent back upon which, like a table, he has gazed for so many hours. He rears in the darkness to admire it. He had forgotten. Every minute of the day seems to have converged. He wants to slow them, to have this sweet ending last.

28

Over France a great summer rain, battering the trees, making the foliage ring like tin. The walls grow dark with water. The gutters are running, the streets all abandoned. It started at dusk. By nine it is still pouring down.

They are in Dole. They stare out the window of a plain café where they have been sitting for an hour or more. Across from them is an empty park, not very large. In it a strange apparatus is being erected. A high wire. Two tall poles have been guyed to the ground. Men are still working in the rain, testing the lights. From time to time the façade of buildings opposite appears in the blue floods, but the wire itself, strung in the upper dark, is invisible. Over the rooftops, like flowers, fireworks burst without sound.

It's a local *fête.* There would have been a crowd, but the rain has kept them away. Only a few families huddle beneath the awnings now. Others sit inside cars. The lights go off again. The square is in darkness.

The café is not empty. There's a table with three men and also, in a raincoat, white legs showing beneath it, the acrobat, who waits at the bar. His face is hard. He's been there for a long time. After a while, the *patron* offered him a drink. *Merci.* The glass is empty now. He stands there quite alone, a man in his thirties, the coat hung over his shoulders.

In a low voice running like a secret, Anne-Marie begins to describe him. He comes from the city, a poor section of Paris, she knows it well. He has a daughter, she explains, a little girl who travels with him, the mother has run away. They journey all over France together, only the two of them. The cheapest hotels. The little girl has no friends, just her father, and for toys a single doll. She's always quiet. She never speaks. Dean doesn't recognize this famous story. He glances at the weary face of the man; upstairs the child is sleeping. It's all bitterly real to him, a fiction for which a place already existed in his heart.

Outside, they have finished the preparations. They come into the café to say this. Somehow the acrobat seems strangely disinterested, nor do they stay to keep him company. One has the feeling that someone else exists, an impresario, an unseen man whom they all obey.

The acrobat has accepted another drink. Dean watches cautiously, afraid of what he sees. Premonitions of disaster come over him. The entire machinery: strings of colored lights along the guy wires, the slender poles rising high into darkness, the invisible platforms—it is all a death they are arranging. He is certain of it. He can feel it in his chest.

The acrobat has said nothing, not a word. He has hardly moved. One loves him for this passivity, this resignation, and for his face which has a gypsy darkness. If it continues to rain there can be no performance, and the rain falls heavily, seldom shifting, drumming on the drenched cloth of the car outside. Only a few people still wait.

Dean counts out the money for the bill. The franc pieces seem unusually bright. He lays them in the saucer. They make a little clicking sound, like teeth, a clear sound, and in that instant he becomes aware it has been heard by, has awakened the solitary dreamer at the bar— he glances up but no, the acrobat has not noticed. He is gazing into the mirror. His white-stockinged legs, powder white, are crossed at the ankle. His slippers are frayed, but he is more than he seems, this man. He is an agent, an emissary. He has selected a disguise in which he moves nervously, white as a moth in the spotlight above the common crowds, but it is all a conceit. He is far more important than that. Dean knows this. He recognizes it— impossible to explain. It really does not even concern her. It is all meant for him, and when it is announced that the performance has been cancelled, Dean receives the news without surprise. It makes no difference. The performance itself was incidental.

"Wait here," he says. "I'll get the car."

He vanishes into the rain. Anne-Marie stands just inside the door until the car pulls up with that vast, irregular grace, its headlights yellow and reflecting in the windows of the café, the wipers ticking slowly. She runs for it. He leans across the seat to hold the door open. His face is wet, his hair. She gets in hurriedly.

"What rain!" she says.

Dean doesn't drive off. Instead, he tries to look through the running glass, to see inside the café one last time. The bar is empty. The acrobat has gone.

They drive through the streets of an unknown town. The rain pours down like gravel. In the green light of the instrument panel he feels as homeless, as desolate as a criminal. Gently she wipes his wet cheeks with her fingers. They have nowhere to go. They are strangers here, the doors of the town are closed to them. Suddenly he is filled with intimations of being found somehow, of being seized and taken away. He doesn't even have a chance to talk to her. They are separated. They are lost to each other. He tries to cry out in this coalescing dream, to tell her where she should go, what she should do, but it's too complicated. He cannot. She is gone.

A genuine desperation overwhelms him. He hasn't the money to really go off with her. They are imprisoned in the smallness of Autun, a night or two away doesn't matter, and now, yes, he knows it, they have been discovered. Dean is sure of this. And I, too, in retrospect, I see he was right. The acrobat has disappeared into the villages of France, into the night of all Europe, perhaps. The Delage is alone on the streets. One need not follow as it crawls through the darkness—it can be recognized anywhere.

Dean is dispirited. In the hotel room he undresses carefully, laying them down as if the clothes are not his, as if they are to be burned. The night is cool with all its rain and a chill passes over his nakedness. He feels lean as an orphan. The past has vanished and he fears the future. His money is lying on the table, and in the dark he goes over to count it, the paper bills only. He lifts the folded notes. The coins spill off, and one falls to the floor, rolls away. He listens but cannot tell in which direction it has gone. Anne-Marie comes up behind him, naked too, and suddenly he is transfixed, like a hare in the headlights of a car. Her arms steal around him. Her body touching him, the points of her breasts, the soft bed of hair, is a virtual agony. They caress one another, pale as embryos in the dark.

She wants to be arranged over a chair. Dean finds

one. She bends over it. Her breasts hang sweetly, like the low boughs of a tree, like handfuls of money. His hands slide to her waist which is narrow. He begins slowly, and she breathes as if sinking into a bath. From without is the sound of pouring rain.

In the morning it is calm. He awakens as if a fever has passed. Europe has returned to its real proportions. The immortal cities swim in sunlight. The great rivers flow. His prick is large and her hand moves to it as soon as her eyes open. He searches his clothing for the crumpled, leaden tube. He hands it to her. She looks at it impassively. He kicks the covers away as she unscrews the cap. She begins to spread it on. The coolness makes him jump. Afterwards she rolls over and in the full daylight he slowly inserts this gleaming declaration. Her forehead is pressed to the sheet. Her eyes are closed. Dean barely notices. Finally he is entered all the way. He lies still.

"Would you like to read?" he says.

"Comment?"

"Read. A magazine."

"Yes," she answers vaguely.

They move to the edge of the bed. There is an old copy of *Réalités*. He reaches for it and pulls it to the floor. Her head leaning down, she starts to turn the pages. Dean looks over her shoulder. It is Sunday morning. Ten o'-clock. Only the occasional, soft leafing of paper interrupts the stillness. She has come to an article about the paintings of Bonnard. They read it together. He waits until she has finished the page. Gently he begins.

"Not enough *graisse*," she says.

He withdraws carefully—she is almost clinging to him, it feels—and she applies a bit more, wiping her fingers afterwards on the sheet. In it goes—she lies calm—and intrigued by a page that shows photographs of the fourteen kinds of feminine appeal (innocence, mystery, naturalness, etc.), he begins to move in and out in long, delirious strokes. France is bathed in sunshine. The shops are closed. Churches are filled. In every town, behind locked doors, the restaurants are laying their tables, preparing for lunch.

29

The more clearly one sees this world, the more one is obliged to pretend it does not exist. It was strange how I found myself almost completely silent when I was with her. There was everything to talk about it seemed, but we simply could never begin. I took her to dinner in May when Dean went to Paris for a few days, and what days they were, summery, vast. The light failed slowly. The world was filled with blue cities, fragrant, mysterious. We dined at the hotel. From time to time I smiled at her, like a stupid uncle, while she talked about Dean. I was really not too interested. The terms of the encounter were all wrong. I knew what she was. I was ready to confess, to fall to my knees like a believer. It would have been a terrible moment. She would have denied it all. More likely, she wouldn't have understood. What she wants is to know what his father and sister will think of her. Will they find her nice?

"I'm sure they will," I say.

"He doesn't talk about his father."

"Well, his father's a critic—you know that. Rather elegant man, I gather."

"*Pardon.*"

"I say he's very elegant, very social."

"Still," she says, "he could find me nice."

"Of course." Why am I not telling her the truth?

We sit over *salade de tomates,* the rich slices specked with parsley fragments, gleaming with oil. I wonder if she feels herself ordinary. Does she know that his sister wanted to come down here to see him but Dean insisted on meeting her in Paris? Yes, of course she knows. She knows everything, sometimes I am convinced. Anyway, the future doesn't surprise her. Much of it exists already—I have said that before.

"Some more *tomates?*" she says, offering to serve me.

She helps herself. Her mouth glistens. Across from us is an English couple. They're both very young. He has dry, red hair. She is thin-faced and shy. Her dress looks like wallpaper, and they sit in an utter, English silence reading the menu as if it were a contract. In an accent so perfect it surprises me, Anne-Marie whispers,

"Did I hurt you, darling?"

"What?"

It's a line from a joke Dean's told her. Her face is full of a mischievous joy. But I don't know the original story. She delivers it with the assurance of a clown. That's what *he* says, she explains. They're in bed together. Then *she* says: no, why? And he says: you moved. Her smile is questioning.

"Do I tell it right?" she asks. She looks to see if I am amused. I love her contempt for the sexual life of the English.

Dean is at the Calais, his car parked in the huge square past the corner with a white violation slip already tucked under the wiper. He's sharing a room with his sister and being very agreeable. He desperately needs money—everything depends on it—and she wants to talk about his life, his future life, that is. She knows he'll be touchy.

"Now don't get angry . . ." she says.

"Oh, Amy . . ." he begins. He knows exactly how. She

plays every card face up like a woman surrendering to love. He's perfectly ready to face this future life, Dean says. More than that, it's already appearing before him. These months have made an enormous difference. They've been like the wilderness for him, how can he explain it? Suddenly she wants to embrace him. She feels relieved and a little guilty.

"Do you mean it?"

"It's changed my life," he says. "It's changing my life." He smiles. He loves her. Sometimes she is like a toy.

"But what have you been doing?"

"Seeing no one," he says. "Living the life of a little town. It's like saying: stop all this, stop the noise; now, what should it all look like?"

"Yes . . ." she agrees.

"Life is composed of certain basic elements," he says. "Of course, there are a lot of impurities, that's what's misleading."

He has always instructed her. She listens gravely.

"What I'm saying may sound mystical, but in everybody, Ame, in all of us, there's the desire to find those elements somehow, to discover them, you know? Sometimes I think they're the same for all of us, but maybe they're not. I mean, we look at the Greeks and say, ah, they built this civilization, this whole brilliant world, out of certain, simple things. Why can't we? And if not a civilization, why can't each of us, properly directed, build a life, I mean a happy life? Believe me, the elements exist. When you enter certain rooms, when you look at certain faces, suddenly you realize you're in the presence of them. Do you know what I mean?"

"Of course, I do," she says. "If you could achieve that, you'd have everything."

"And without it you have . . ." he shrugs, "a life."

"Like everybody's."

"Just like everybody's," he says.

"I don't want that."

"Neither do I."

"I can never tell when you're conning me," she says.
He shakes his head slowly.

"I'm not," he promises. "Because I want you to do
me a tremendous favor."

"What?"

He doesn't answer.

"Later," he says.

She goes into the bathroom to finish dressing. Dean
reads a magazine. She comes out to comb her hair.

"Where shall we go?" she says.

"Shall we have a good dinner?"

"All right. But not too expensive." The phrase worries him. He tries to ignore it.

"It's on me," he says.

"Do you have any money? Daddy said you were desperate."

"Me?"

"Yes."

"No," he says. "I have a job."

"You have? What?"

"Tutoring," he says.

"You never said anything about that."

"Well, it's not exactly making me rich."

"He made me promise not to give you any money, no
matter what. He was sure you were going to ask me for
some."

"He acts like I'm your no-good husband."

"No. He worries about you."

"His methods are curious," Dean says. "Besides, I
hate lessons about the value of money. What's the point?
Everybody knows it's valuable. I don't want any lessons
imposed on me. I don't like people that give lessons.

We're all free. We were meant to love and help each other, not to give lessons."

"No," she says, "I think he just wants you to . . ."

"What?"

"Have a more regular life," she decides.

Dean smiles.

"Come on," he says. "Are you ready?"

They go down one floor in the elevator and walk along the corridor.

"Money," Dean says. "I'll tell you it's very hard to think clearly when you don't have any. That's one of my discoveries. Of course, it's hard when you have too much."

"It certainly is."

"One has to be very careful," Dean says wryly.

His sister knocks on a door.

"Donna? Can we come in?"

"Sure."

It's her roommate at college. Dean finds her very good-looking. A thrilling, wide mouth, grey eyes. A slim girl, like a runner. She's interested in him. She knows he went to Yale. Did he know Larry Troy, she asks? Questions like that. He responds with soft, almost uncertain no's.

"What class were you?" she says.

"Several."

When he tells her he never finished, she emits a small: oh. But it takes courage to do that, she adds, to set out on your own. Only a real individual . . . Dean nods. He's heard all this before.

They walk down the street together. The sidewalk is very wide. The *place* itself, filled with parked cars, seems tremendous. Lost in these rich dimensions, they cut across towards the Delage. Dean takes the ticket from the windshield and begins to read it.

"What's that?" his sister asks.

He shrugs.

"Is it for parking?" she says. "You don't have to pay it. You're only visiting."

"Say, what kind of great car is this?" Donna says.

"Do you like it?"

"I love it," she says. "It's very you."

"You think so?"

"Absolutely," she says.

The glittering night of Paris receives them. Darkness has restored the old car's elegance, and down the boulevards they float to a restaurant near the Invalides. The dinner costs eighty-five francs. Dean's last money. He nevertheless leaves a large tip. He does it mechanically, without caring, pure as a gambler who has lost. They walk along the Champs, have a coffee, and end the night above the city at Sacré-Coeur. At her floor, Donna says,

"It was such a great evening. It's the best evening we've had on the whole tour."

"I wish I could have shown you more of Paris."

"Oh," she says, "I do, too."

"Next time."

"I just wish we were staying," she says.

She walks slowly down the hallway, the key dangling like an ornament from her hand.

In the morning everything seems different. His confidence has gone cold. They are talking, over breakfast, of how they will spend the day. Everybody's going to Versailles, but if they decide to go, too, she'd rather drive out in his car. Or perhaps they should just go off by themselves, the two of them. And take Donna, if he likes. Dean wants to ask for money, now—he can't go through the day otherwise—but the beginning of her reply terrifies him. He can hear her saying: you know how much I love you . . . I'd do anything . . .

"Amy," he says, "all kidding aside . . ."

"What?"

"I *am* desperate."

She looks at him, a little uncertain.

"I need money," he says.

"Oh."

"I sold my ticket."

"You really did?"

"I had to."

"Daddy will give it back to you," she says.

"I don't want him to find out. I need three hundred and fifty dollars."

She seems embarrassed by her reply.

"I don't have it," she says.

"How much do you have?"

"I don't know. I really don't know."

"Listen, forget that. I'm serious. I mean it, Amy, my need is . . . I need the money. I need it to get home."

"How much do you really need?"

"Three hundred and fifty dollars," he says.

"I only have a hundred. I only have traveler's checks."

"I have to have more than that, baby."

"I don't have it."

"Can you borrow it?" he says.

"Be honest. Are you in trouble?"

"No, no." He sighs. He looks at her and then at the table. "Do you think you can borrow it? How about Donna?"

"Are you ever going to pay it back?"

"Certainly."

"I just can't ask her for two hundred and fifty dollars, just like that."

"She may have part of it," Dean says.

"You're not in any trouble?"

"No, I deeply, sincerely need some money, but I'm not in any trouble. I'll be in trouble if I don't get it."

"Then it's true?"

"No, I'm only kidding. Listen, how about asking Donna? She'll lend you money, won't she?"

"I suppose so," she says.

"You've got to do it for me," Dean tells her.

In the dusk at Orly they part. From the upper platform, Dean watches her mount the steps. She pauses at the top. A final wave. This long, polished tube with its comfortable seats is the jet to America. He feels a moment of great loneliness. He would like to be on board, sitting down beside them. He hates the thought of walking out to the car by himself. Life seems to be fleeing from him.

The door closes, is sealed. A period of deathlike silence, and the engines start. Inside they are unfolding newspapers. It begins to move. He tries to identify her at one of the windows. He's too far off. The faces are indistinct. He watches as the plane follows a long, ceremonial path to the runway. It turns. It begins to flow. Once in the air it moves serenely, almost ominously, heeling over without warning, coming level again, following invisible courses into the sky.

He counts the money. Three hundred and fifteen dollars, almost none of it in francs. He folds it carefully and puts it back in his pocket. She's promised to send him fifty more.

The Delage moves in long, steady thrusts, slowing only in towns. He's not at all tired. The trip, it seems, is the shortest ever. He passes everything without even slowing, swinging out and rushing by, uphill and down. Finally he arrives. It's just past eleven, the houses are dark. He runs up the stairs like a cat and knocks lightly. She is waiting.

30

I n the street, in the earliest morning, the car lies open, like a boat. The town is a harbor; the water is like glass. There is not a creak, not a cough as they ease along silent passages, the engine idling. In the country, luminous but still awaiting sunlight, the air is cool and sweet. They drive without speaking. They're still sleepy. After twenty kilometers, Anne-Marie forms a single word.

"*Alors.*"

"What's wrong?"

She's forgotten the jacket to her suit.

"Oh, Christ," Dean says.

It's back in the room. He slows down and stops on the grass shoulder.

"No," she says.

"You want to go back and get it?"

She shakes her head,

"No."

He starts off again, slowly. She shrugs helplessly. She doesn't want to look at him.

"Are you sure?" he says.

"Yes," she says. "We are started."

"It's a great start."

She begins to laugh. Finally Dean smiles. Their last trip. They flash down the tunnels of trees, and the towns unfold before them, flat at first and still sleeping but then with cats, a few people, and by the time they reach Or-léans it's full morning. A large, impressive city. The day is going to be hot. Dean runs across the square to buy some bread and butter. They eat parked in the sunlight, green busses rumbling past, the tourists strolling by in short pants. Bread crumbs are falling into her lap. She has never looked more pleased, more accustomed to seats of real leather, trips to the sea. She squints in the morning brightness. She moves her legs—the leather is hot.

They are really married. That night she will say as much to him: they have picked a good time, when it is safe to make love, and started life together that day. It is in Angers. They are walking the streets after dinner. The city seems foreign to Dean, redolent of Spain, dusty, smelling of trees. The sidewalks are laid between flats of bare earth. It doesn't seem France. Even the cafés are strange, and the couples speak a language he cannot understand.

They have toured the *châteaux* that day. For two francs they can follow a guide who recites a little history as they pass through the great rooms. There are white-haired couples in the crowd, tourists in sandals, school-teachers. An American woman and her two daughters in linen dresses. Someone is whispering in German. The guide promptly forces a translation of the tour into their hands, like a menu. They protest. They understand French, they say. The guide only smiles. Dean stands at the edge of the group. Anne-Marie has gone a little ahead.

"Phillipe," she calls, "come!"

The guide is moving on. Everybody follows.

"Parle français!" Dean whispers when he is close.

"Why?"

She is being playful. They walk out on the balcony that runs the steep face of the building. They are at Amboise, far above the town. Dean refuses to talk. He doesn't want to be taken for an American. He doesn't want to be given a translation by the guide who is now explaining what was enacted here in centuries past. Anne-Marie winces.

"Awful," she says. The road is hundreds of feet below. Protestants about to be hung would see a whole realm before them, sky, wide river, the roofs of the town. "They were more cruel in those days."

"I'd love to have seen it," Dean says.

"Don't. It makes me sick."

One of the daughters has heard them. Her head turns. He sees her whisper to her mother. He tries to lag behind, but Anne-Marie will not let him.

"Phillipe, come on," she says.

"I'll kill you!" he whispers.

She only smiles.

They arrive in Angers tired, in the midst of evening traffic. People are shopping and driving home from work. A cool smell of foliage fills the air, the trace of flowers. They find a small hotel. The entrance is on a narrow street—after they unload their luggage, he must go somewhere and park.

Dean feels a slight chill as he draws the bedspread over him. Perhaps it was the sun. He lies quite still. The room is bare. He recognizes nothing in it, not a color, not a line. Suddenly he becomes frightened. He begins to count his money mentally. He's left some of it behind, five hundred francs, and there was a garage bill for tuning the engine. They bought some clothes. He adds it up. He decides to put two hundred francs under the floormat of the car. That will leave about seven hundred—he adds it again—it will be close. It's forty or fifty every time they get gas. He tries to calculate the mileage. Perhaps they shouldn't try to go so far.

His eyes open a little at the sound of the key. Anne-Marie has been taking a bath. She's wearing his cotton robe. When she stands near the bed she unties it. It opens, falls away. The sight of her fresh nakedness frightens him even more. Suddenly it is quite clear how acrobatic, how dangerous everything is. It seems not to be his own life he is living, but another, the life of some victim. It will all collapse. He will have to find work, pay rent, walk home every day for lunch. He is weak suddenly, he doesn't believe in himself. She slips into the bed. A virtual panic comes over him. He lies motionless, his eyes closed.

"*Tu dors?*" she says softly.

He doesn't know what to answer.

"No," he breathes. After a moment he adds, "I have a little headache."

"Poor child." She strokes his cheek. He manages a papery smile.

The dinner revives him somewhat. She even has two glasses of wine, but then, it's an occasion. Afterwards they walk along the avenue, beneath the dark trees. They come to a large store, closed, of course, but fully lighted. Couples linger before the displays, refrigerators, rows of them, doors open, cardboard arrows pointing out their features.

"Are they more expensive in America?" she asks.

"I've never bought one." His eyes move uncertainly. The model numbers are cabalistic, the prices seem terrifying.

"But you must know."

"Let's go," he says.

"This one I find nice," she says, pointing.

"It's too small."

"No."

"Come on."

"It's big enough," she says.

"Baby, please stop this."

"*Attends.*"

"I don't want to look at them any more. It's boring," he says.

"There's nothing else to do. Where do you want to go? Do you want to go and dance?"

"Yes," he says.

"Ah!" she cries.

"Sure. Come on."

They begin to walk and in the end have come back to the hotel. The dining room is dark. The desk seems empty.

"Do you want to ask?" he says.

"No," she says. "It's late."

He takes their key from the little board, and they walk up the carpeted stairs. The room seems plainer than before. He brushes his teeth. He is ready to sleep.

"*Non*," she says. One doesn't begin a married life like that.

"I'm really tired."

"Maybe for dancing," she says.

He may not be interested, but she knows what is best for him. It's like a bowl of hot soup. She makes him undress and lie down with her. She starts to caress him, he cannot escape her hands. Finally he begins, obediently, to make love, working himself in from side to side like a lever. It's a little dry, this prescription, but she suffers it. She knows a woman must be prepared for that.

In the morning light enters through the thin curtains. She has hold of his prick. She kisses it sweetly to start the day. It is hers now, she says.

----------------- *31* -----------------

D ays of marriage. They live in connubial bliss above the sea. The room is small, but there is a balcony and beneath it the water breaking softly. The hotel is more than they can afford.

Morning. Her hair streamed across the pillow, the covers drawn up to her chin. Outside, the cries of seabirds float in the still air. *Mon mari,* she calls him. He smiles.

In the dining room they sit near a family with two

sons. The mother is strict with them—they are fifteen years old, sixteen, it's hard to say. They're allowed a little wine, that's all. Most of the time they sit stiffly while the parents talk. She would like a son, Anne-Marie says. The room is filled with the sound of forks, the smell of bread. A son.

Dean is glancing at the family.

"What will his name be?" she says.

"I don't know. What?"

She wants him to guess.

"Jean-Pierre."

"No."

"Maurice? Robert? Not Phillipe?"

"No."

"I give up."

"Dmitri," she says.

He makes a gesture with his hands.

"You faked me out," he says.

"What?"

"You fooled me."

"He will be educated in America until he is eighteen," she says. "Your father was great [she will tell him], but sometimes a little boring."

"A little boring?"

"*Oui.*"

"You mean me?"

She nods.

"It's my son?"

Her reply is soft,

"Of course."

The young boys are watching them, their uncertain glances settling for a moment and then bolting away. Anne-Marie is clever, she can feel their eyes. She knows exactly when to look up and send them scurrying.

Days of marriage by the sea. They walk far out on the

rocks, the hotels, the curve of beach passing from view as
they turn the point. They come to a large, flat block
around which the sea boils, sucking and running, welling
up in the faults. She removes the top of her suit and lies
down, first on her stomach, twenty minutes later on her
back. The sun's silence seems to overcome the noise of
water. Dean's skin is a kind that turns dark quickly. His
lips crack a little, but his eyes are white, his teeth. His face
takes on a hardwood brilliance. His limbs seem stronger.
Beneath his trunks is a white like fresh bandages. His buttocks are like the inside of an apple.

"You are lovely," she says.

They are making love afterwards, burned a little,
their flesh tasting of salt. The room seems still, like a
school after hours. On the bidet, she farts, a tiny, delicious
sound. She is embarrassed.

"*Pardon,*" she says.

Silence. Dean's eyes are closed. He says nothing. She
wonders if he has fallen asleep. She glances around the
partition. Dean lies very still, but he cannot prevent a
smile. She gets in bed again and covers up. She feels a little sick, she tells him. Her period is coming.

"Good," he says.

They sit through elaborate meals, soup, fish, meat,
dessert, fruit, wine, in the long room, always in daylight,
with its gallery of windows beyond which the sea lies silent, the many tables. At night they sleep like birds in a
nest. Rain beats against the windows. Dean gets up to
close them and finds nothing—it's only the sea.

At the casino there's dancing and second-rate films.
They haven't the money to gamble. Anyway, she's too
young. It's on her identity papers. They sit in the empty
salon of the hotel. In the evening darkness, it's like a
great, abandoned liner. Anne-Marie takes all the small
cards out of the deck. She's going to teach him a game. He

tries to listen to the explanation. His face feels tight, like dried paper. His eyes move distractedly from one thing to another. He yawns. He can see the wide, carpeted stairway and the people slowly ascending. The family comes in, from the cinema probably, and goes up, the boys looking dejected, absolutely spiritless. The light is dim. After a while his eyes begin to ache from staring at the numbers on the cards. The symbols are ugly. The black of the spades seems to be running. The hearts have turned blue. With the sad insistence of a tent flapping, the edge of the sea curls on the shore, curls and falls. As he listens, the sound seems to swell, to become broader, to overwhelm everything.

Along the dim corridor they walk, the floor groaning under their feet. There is no music from the closed doors, no voices. The sheets are damp. Nights of marriage. Dean is worried about the salt air ruining the chrome of the car. He should have coated it with something. There's no garage—it's parked behind the hotel, covered with moisture. In the morning the sun dries it off.

They stay six days, talking to no one, walking the steep, piney roads to the upper town, passing large, family villas, dark and silent, arranged on the hillside to face the sea. The grounds of these houses are beautiful, hidden by dense trees.

They are like invalids. Their hours are long and uneventful. They eat three times a day. In the mornings, on the way to the W.C. the hall is lined with breakfast trays, napkins soiled, rolls broken, abandoned outside the doors. The patients have already gone out, walking slowly in the sunlight. Years of marriage. After breakfast it is quite a long time until lunch, and after lunch, the whole afternoon . . . On the beach in front of the hotel the cries of children rise shrill as birds'. Anne-Marie walks naked around the room. Her bare feet make no noise. Her tampon has a bit of white string which hangs, curled a little, between her legs. Her breasts are pale, but not white. It is only her loins which are emblazoned so brilliantly it seems like a garment.

In the early morning, elated just to be putting their things in the car again—Dean lowers the top, the interior brims with sunlight—they leave.

32

At night they come to a strange, *démodé* town, like a great sanitarium: Bagnoles. France is dotted with aging spas, their days of elegance long past, the damp hotels no longer filled, the voices vanished, the ceremonies of an idle life. They enter on curving roads, past the silent lake. The buildings all seem empty. It's like a great estate, the master of which has disappeared. Still, it's kept open, it continues an existence exactly as if he were there. It's like an old letter, a suite in which an heiress has died.

Graceful as a bird they circle in the dusk, passing the worn façades: the Gayot, Terrasse, Castel, Bois Joli. The shops are closed. The trees have turned black. Not a soul on the dim streets, not a sound except that of the car. The casino is bleak and forbidding, its green chairs abandoned, its curtains drawn. The silence of woods at evening, of still waters, is everywhere. After the second time around, Dean stops.

"It's depressing," he says. He reaches for the book. "We can go on to Alençon. How big is that?"

She looks it up.

"Vingt-sept mille."

"How about hotels?"

"There's not much."

"Not a single decent one?"

"There's a hospital for the insane."

"Let me see."

He tries to read. The light is almost gone.

"Well, we could go on to Paris," he says. "It's about three hours."

She shrugs.

"*Comme tu veux,*" she says.

He begins to turn the pages.

"But can we eat here?" she says.

"Hm?" He's still reading. "All right. We'll decide afterwards."

It's a long meal. There's only one waiter in the restaurant. He's like a veteran of Fort Douaumont. For him, everything ended long ago. He disappears into the kitchen for ten minutes and then comes out with the bread. There's a door that opens to the street and another into the hotel. In the end this is the one they take. It's too late to go on. The lobby is dark. The keys, hung on a varnished honeycomb of wood, are almost all in place. They walk up carpeted stairs—there is no sound—to what can only be called a chamber. Walls of a cream that has turned to ocher, heavy wine drapes. In the ceiling fixture the bulbs are clear glass. It is threatening, this room. The air is stale.

Dean opens the balcony doors. Silence. Across the black lake the casino is alight now, the one ornament in a darkness hung like curtains. No one seems to go in or out. The placards announce films, concerts, to the empty street.

They walk around for a while. There is the scent of a killing boredom in the air. One can recognize it, like mould. The prospect of a few hours is enough to seem terrifying. They buy tickets for the movie. The cashier detaches them from a large roll. There are a few people already inside—that's something, at least. They are saved. They sit quietly, waiting for the lights to dim. Nobody even whispers. Finally it begins. The screen becomes luminous. Music, voices, images born on the shifting pales of light.

On the way back to the hotel they discover that a few shops have opened late, and they pause at the window of an *antiquaire*. It's like a museum. Not a single client. Among the gilded pieces they suddenly see the white of a face, the owner, a woman, pale as a mourner.

It is only after the door to the room closes and he turns the key that Dean feels anything other than death. Even so, there is something artificial and dense about the furnishings, the inadequate light. The doors to the balcony have been shut. Through the glass he can see that a flexible, wooden blind has been drawn completely down. The covers of the bed have been folded back to reveal a clinical white. She is talking about the film. He hears nothing. He merely watches, intrigued by the smallest movement she makes, fascinated by the shape of her calf.

She stands naked, her legs together, brushing her teeth before the sink. Dean is watching her carefully. From where he sits, he reaches out and touches her. There is no authority in the gesture. It is an act of reassurance—he is fixing reality. She puts the toothbrush down. She doesn't like to look closely at her teeth. She dries the corners of her mouth with the towel and then applies some cream. Her eyes meet his for a moment in the mirror. She is not certain what he is thinking or what he is about to do. But he's not prepared to talk, that's obvious to her.

She lies in bed with her eyes open, waiting. Dean undresses. He moves about the room, glancing at her from time to time. Finally he smiles. She does not return it. She has prepared herself for an obedience that cannot be so

162   *JAMES SALTER*

easily released. Her face is solemn, almost rebellious. He
opens the balcony doors but doesn't raise the blind. He
turns out the light. In the bed she moves to his side immediately, as if released by the darkness. Her hands, those
thin hands, swim down his body. Dean lies motionless.
His silence, his stillness please her. They define her existence. She must conquer them. Of course, it is only a
game. He is merely waiting, adorned in a sort of cruelty
which excites her and which she must beg him, without
speaking a word, to forget. His heart is beating faster. He
feels his prick grow an inch or more beneath her touch.
The vaseline is chilly as she applies it with great care.
Dean is breathing like a runner before a race. He is thinking of the waiters in the casino, the audience at the cinema, the dark hotels as she lies on her stomach and with
the ease of sitting down at a well-laid table, but no more
than that, he introduces himself. They lie on their sides.
He tries not to move. There are only the little, invisible
twitches, like a nibbling of fish. In the midst of them he
falls asleep. Then she does, too, and like this, together,
they pass the night. The final night of the journey.

33

They arrive home on Sunday evening, weary from
traffic. The roads are crowded. For half an hour
Dean has been dogging the pale of his headlights
which now, in the narrow streets, begin to show bright.
It's like driving under water. A green twilight gleams far
above. He turns the last corner. The great, battered truck
of the Corsicans is parked among the strewn wrappings,
the marvelous rotting odors. As he pulls in, the headlights reflect on the glass of the darkened store. He
switches them off, then the motor. They sit for a moment.

A great joy, a sense of completion comes over him. They gather all her things, and he carries them upstairs. He's anxious to leave her. He's tired of having to be with her all the time.

I find him lying on the bed in blue canvas shoes. His hands are folded behind his head. The radio is playing. It feels good to be back, he tells me. It really does.

He looks black as an Egyptian. When he smiles his teeth seem to leap out of his sunburned face. We swim in a faint aroma, a bouquet of music as he talks.

"Well, where did you go?"

"Everywhere," he says. "Angers. Orléans. Perros-Guirec. We really drove."

"Was it nice?"

"It's a beautiful country," he says quietly. He begins to tell me about it, the sea with its rocks, the old hotel. He describes the Loire, the haunted evening in Bagnoles. He is talking almost compulsively. All the details come forth, descriptions, feelings, smells. He falls silent, gathers things, goes on. Somehow I have the impression that he is laying it all before me, the essence of this glorious life he has spent in France. He is setting the past in order. There are certain things which should be confessed, and he knows I am interested. Nothing he says is exceptional, but I recognize the events. I understand everything we are not saying.

"How's Anne-Marie?"

"She's as tan as I am. You ought to see her," he says. "She looks great."

"You're the color of teak."

"We had beautiful weather," he says. "Almost every day. And we ate. We sat at the table like an old French couple, you know, just eating. And we made love every night. But the sun, you really can't believe what good sun we had."

He pulls his shirt out to show me the line. He grins.

He is invincible. It's like a game of chess in which his pieces continually overpower me, but we have long ceased to contest.

He begins to wander around the room while he talks. His clothing is scattered everywhere. He goes into the bathroom and discovers some lotion which he slowly rubs into his face, especially around his mouth. He lies down again. That lean face, dark as a farm boy's. It has an edge to it. The bones seem able to cut right through me. He gets up again and begins to look through his suitcase. There's an apple among his clothes. He offers me half.

"No, thanks. Didn't you eat?"

"No. Just lunch."

He lies supine, the pillow doubled beneath his neck. I listen to the moist explosion of his teeth in the hard flesh.

"I'm too tired to eat," he says.

"Come on. I haven't had anything."

"I'm really not hungry," he says.

He picks around the core, getting the last flecks with little incisions of his teeth. When he finishes, he lays it on a magazine. He stares at the ceiling.

"I may be leaving," he says.

An enormous silence which I am finally obliged to break.

"Oh, really?"

"I think so."

"Where will you be going?"

"America," he says. "Home."

"I see. Alone?"

"Oh, sure," he says. "I mean, I'm coming back."

"I see."

I can't think of what to say.

"Well . . ." I begin.

"You know, I just have to go home for a while. I don't have any money. I've been hanging on ever since last fall, and I can't any more. You get to the point where you just can't. So I have to go back and . . ." he sighs, ". . . talk to my father. Well, more than that. I have to organize myself a little. I've even been thinking about going back to school."

"Back to Yale?"

"Oh, I couldn't get back in. Some smaller college. NYU maybe."

"Smaller?"

"Well, I didn't mean it that way," he says. "I really haven't thought about where."

"No."

Then, as if commenting, he allows himself the briefest of laughs.

"The only thing is," he says, "uh, I'm a little short of money."

"Of course."

"I don't have quite enough for the ticket." He pauses. "So, I was wondering . . ."

"How much would it be?" I ask.

"I'd leave you the car, you know, if anything happened . . ."

"The car? But it's not your car."

"Yes, it is," he says.

"I thought it belonged to some friend."

"No, no, he gave it to me. I can even get a letter from him if I have to."

I know it's not true. He's simply out of money, like a gambler, and he must be supplied. I hurriedly try to think of a phrase to help me refuse him, but I can't. If I were to deny him . . . anyway, it wouldn't make that much difference. He would go on. Besides, I cannot make such a decision. He isn't subject to judgments of mine—and I have the money.

"I need about three hundred dollars," he says.

"Three hundred."

"Can you let me have that much? I mean, against the Delage, of course."

"Well . . . Yes, I guess so."

"Oh," he says, his head falls back, "listen, you're a great guy."

Yes, and I find myself believing it even though I am helping prepare his escape. The act is somehow criminal. It is something I will be ashamed of later. I am only exchanging his disgust for my own.

"How long will you be gone?"

"I don't know," he says. "I honestly don't. Not long. Maybe a month or so, I'm not sure."

"Well, if you really go back to school . . ."

"That's right, it would be much longer. Of course, that's only a possibility."

". . . you wouldn't be back."

"Oh, don't worry. If that happens, I'll send you the money. I mean, I can get it easily enough. Even if I had to take it out of tuition or something. It wouldn't make any difference."

"I'm not worried. It's not that. The whole thing surprises me, that's all."

"You thought I was getting married," he says.

"No."

"I might."

"Really?"

"I've thought about it," he says.

"I suppose so."

He jumps up. The promise of money has given him an appetite. We go down towards the Champ, walking along the blank streets. Autun is silent, but it sleeps like an ancient woman. It hears every scrap of sound without even waking. It is ageless. It can see in the dark.

Buried among other buildings deep in the town—

there are alleys one can pass by, cats know the way—above the level of trees and black foliage, the mysterious fragrance, the movement of branches, in a room filled with this same cool air of evening she lies asleep, her pale arms fallen, her lips apart. The varnished, orange doors of the *armoire* are closed, and a towel is hung, unfolded, by the sink. Her toothbrush—my finger dares to touch it lightly—is no longer damp. On the floor clothes are dropped. I can see her shoes, her limp stockings. Finally I glance at her, and the blood drops out of my heart; her eyes are not shut. She is staring at me. The pure, young white of her eyes, that blue white—I am found by it.

I even have a premonition that we are going to meet her as we walk down for a sandwich. It frightens me. I'm sure she could read what we have done in my face. I am ready to confess it all, I haven't the slightest instinct to escape or lie, but Dean, ah, he would greet her with a smile. The whole difference lies in that. I am not strong enough to love her. One must be selfish.

Watching him eat, I am plagued by this. Gradually I sink into a fine, a delicate hatred. I no longer hear what he says. I am only conscious of my own thoughts and the sound of his teeth chewing bread. He reeks of assurance. We are all at his mercy. We are subject to his friendship, his love. It is the principles of his world to which we respond, which we seek to find in ourselves. It is his power which I cannot even identify, which is flickering, sometimes present and sometimes not—without it he is empty, a body without breath, as ordinary as my own reflection in the mirror—it is this power which guarantees his existence, even afterwards, even when he is gone.

34

He will return for her. Silence. She looks at him. Then a single word,
"*Non.*"
"Yes."
"*Non,*" she says flatly.

Well, then, he can't explain it, he says. If she's going to insist that she knows . . . She sits watching him, her mouth drawn down, her eyes suspicious. He will send for her, he says.

"When?"

"I don't know exactly. I have to get the fare."

"What?"

"The fare. The money for the ticket."

A quick, bitter shrug.

"Will you just listen?" he says.

She says nothing.

"I don't have it right now," he explains.

Her face seems softer, but there is no understanding in it, or at least no agreement. She looks at the floor.

"Listen, I swear to you," he says. He raises his hand.

She glances up.

"Really," he says.

"On the head of your mother?"

"Yes."

She motions with her chin.

"What?"

"Say it," she says.

"On the head of my mother."

She sighs. He is sitting beside her on the bed. He lies back and begins to talk of what it will be like. At first she resists, but then he can tell from the way the sound of his voice vanishes, from her very stillness, that she is listen-

168

ing. They will go all over the city, he will show her every part of it. They will walk the great avenues, look in all the stores. Saturday night they stay out very late and go dancing. She has only two kinds of clothes: slacks and a *pull* to live in—corduroys for him—and one marvelous dress to go out in. Two, he corrects, one for the afternoon, another for evening. And he has a single, fine suit, very dark, grey, black maybe. A bed. A table. A few chairs. Their windows look out on a bridge.

They lie still, breathing softly, their heads on the long bolster still enclosed in its flowered case. The shutters are drawn. Noon has fallen. There is the faint clatter of plates and beyond that, a ritual silence. A radio, perhaps. An occasional car. They sleep.

They awake in a different world. Dean's eyes drift about vaguely, finally falling upon the clock. An hour has passed. He sits up and quietly begins to remove his clothes, shoes first, then socks. The floor is cool and pleasant beneath his feet.

They pose naked before the mirror. Dean is taller. His body is dark. He stands a bit to the side, like her shadow. The light enters in thin, level strips, gills, which cross the floor. He slips his prick between her legs from behind and she gives it a little hug. She reaches behind her to stroke his balls with her fingertips. He looks like a lifeguard. There is a small roll of fat, a marble bannister, perched on his hip.

They make love slowly. He fixes her across the dark flowers and works it in as if wedging a log. Then he has her sit astride him. Her voice is invisible, a whisper from the street.

"It feels as if it's touching my heart," she says.

She raises herself slightly, her hands on his waist.

"I think it is," she says.

Dean smiles. He forces her down a bit. She struggles

softly. Then he turns her over and sounds her. It's like a
rain of love. Everywhere his mind turns he is drenched
by it. As if in separate rooms, as if engaged in separate
acts, they occupy themselves until the last instant and afterwards lie collapsed, the bedclothes scattered about
them. Their voices are low, inconsequential. Outside the
window, pigeons lurch across the tiles.

They drive to St. Léger, the sun splashing the depths
of the car, hitting their knees. The streets vanish behind
them. The last curve. They start down the long incline,
through the tunnels brief and cool, descending further,
under the viaduct its empty chambers blue with air, past
the roadsigns and gone. The trees wash by them. The car
accelerates, the great axles cracking, the road flying beneath.

Her mother is happy to see them. At the kitchen table
they sit and talk, the cat passing rhythmically between
Dean's feet, reversing, leaning against his ankles. It is
strangely silent, even with them talking. It's like the corridor of a hospital or an empty ward. Dean feels the glances
of her mother. She looks at him almost shyly. When their
eyes meet, she smiles. Her husband is working. The chair
in which he usually sits near the wall is empty, a wooden
chair with a thin, soiled cushion. Anne-Marie says nothing to her mother about Dean leaving. They talk about the
neighbors, the automobile accidents, clothes. The afternoon is homely with gossip. There is nothing to make one
believe he is seeing this room for the last time.

It is late when they return. Cars are parked in the
square; the birds are making their last flights before dark.
They have dinner at the hotel. The room is crowded. She
is enormously affectionate. It infuses her smallest gestures, her smiles. The meal turns, quite by itself, into an
occasion, a long intermingling of feelings broken by the
arrival of courses. They talk of the past, remembering

various places, difficulties, joys. She has a second glass of wine. Outside, a blue evening has fallen. I have eaten here many times, I know the sound of diners' voices in this large room illuminated by the white of tablecloths, the slow discussions, an occasional laugh. Through it then, when all is finished, I hear the sound of her heels, unhurried, thin, as she finally walks to the door, pauses. The glances follow her like bows. She waits. He comes along after paying, and they go out together to the street. I am left alone at my table—I always imagine this—watching as they turn and pass through the domed room, among the lighted cases, and at last are gone. Unknown lovers. They disappear into the town. I shall never see them again. I sit there. There are at least ten minutes until I can have my dessert. The waiter will have to come, clear away the main course, take my order.

They climb the stairs. The key turns in the door. The simple mechanics of crime. He lies on the bed, naked, as she takes off her eye make-up. There is the sound of water running. Her face is close to the mirror. She can see him in it, extended, one hand resting inside his thigh.

"You are like a dead king," she says.

She opens the shutters wide. The lights flooding upward from the church seem to carry a bar of darkness with them, a core of iron, into the mysterious sky. Dean makes love to her with great tenderness, kissing her shoulders, listening to her breath. It's as if he's never done it before. He tries to memorize her. His hands touch her carefully. His lips form reverent phrases.

Afterwards they lie for a long time in silence. There is nothing. Their poem is scattered about them. The days have fallen everywhere, they have collapsed like cards. The air has a chill in it. He pulls the covers up. She is so perfectly still she seems asleep. He touches her face. It is wet with tears.

T he morning he is to leave, the last morning, comes, as ordinary as any other. They have spent the night together. Dean watches her move about the room, dressing. There is very little to say. Everything is helplessly quiet, unreal. Things seem artificial, actions which are necessary but completely dry. He takes her to work— the town is just stirring—and they park for a few minutes outside. The street is in shadow and quite cool. A few people pass. Finally they say goodbye. Dean starts the car. She stands waiting. He drives off slowly, moving through flats of sunlight that lie along the way. He turns his head. A final wave. The street curves. He is gone.

Suddenly he is driving faster, bursting forth as if from a channel. The air is lucid and sweet. The grey fronts of Autun come alive. On an impulse he stops to buy an orange.

I hear the door open, and he comes in.

"Well . . ." he finally says.

He sits down. He seems filled with resignation. Then he gets up again.

"What time do you leave?"

"In about two hours," he says. "I'm going to leave some things here. Is that all right?"

"I don't know. What do you want me to do with them?" I will not be here long, a few days at the most.

"Nothing. I just don't want to take them with me," he says. "Maybe I'll put them in the car."

"That would be better."

"That's what I'll do."

He offers me some segments of orange. We sit eating them. The cool juice fills our mouths. The seeds are heavy and very white. We spit them into our palms.

172

"Why don't we go and have something down at the station?" he says.

"All right."

"I just have to finish packing a little," he says.

"Do you want me to help you?"

"No. It's nothing much."

I watch while he does the last, few things. We drive to the station and sit outside the hotel in the first, hot sunshine. Tourists are loading their cars.

"How do you feel?"

"I don't know," he says. "A little nervous."

Then he shrugs. After a pause, he adds,

"Excited, I guess."

"I suppose you are."

"It's been a long time," he says. "Do you remember the day when I first came?"

The day he first came . . .

"I thought I might stay a couple of weeks." He laughs. "A couple of weeks. It feels like my whole life."

Yes. It's true. And mine. These long months. It's as if I've been in prison. My ribs show. My flesh is white, so white I'm ashamed to take off my clothes. And with it is a bitterness that soaks in like brine.

The train leaves at eleven-forty. We weigh his bags in the station. Twenty-two kilos. We multiply it out, he's a few pounds overweight. When he arrives at the airport he can take some things out and put them in his pockets.

"Except I don't have anything very heavy," he says, thinking.

"Shoes."

"Yes," he says, "that'll look great."

We stand on the empty *quai*, solitary as gulls. The station is desolate. The clock has straight, black hands which jump when they move. Suddenly I am crushed by the simplicity of it all: he is leaving. We are here waiting for the train. It is the final hour.

At last it appears. It's silent at first, even drawing close, and it seems not to be slowing. Then the breath of it touches us. The windows peel by, just above our eyes. They separate, slow, come to a stop. We walk to the door. I follow him on, and we find an empty compartment where we put the bags overhead in the rack. I feel impossibly awkward, but there's not long to wait, a minute or two until the warning whistle. I say goodbye and go down to the platform. The train begins to move. It picks up speed very quickly. I can see him waving. I step back. I wave myself. In that instant I think of her, solitary, her head bent forward to the morning's work. Her face seems ordinary. Her chin is small. M. Hoquetis asks if she is feeling all right. *Oui, monsieur,* she says. Is she certain—she looks ill. She tries to smile. *Non, monsieur.* I cannot imagine what she feels. I can only sense it by her absolute, her utter silence as the train curves, crosses the viaduct high in the morning air.

The Delage sits in sunlight, parked nose in to the curb. I walk around it. The dust of France, black with oil, clings to the brake drums. A film of dead insects coats the lamps. I drive back to the house. It steers like a truck. I imagine people in the cafés to be watching me. I'm a little nervous. Naturally, at the corner it stalls. I try to start it up again. A motorcyclist comes alongside me and stares.

In the middle of the afternoon there is a call from Paris. It's Dean. The connection is poor—his voice sounds very shrill.

"How's Paris?"

"God, it's crowded," he says. "There are a million tourists here."

"Really?"

"You ought to see the cars."

"Did they have your reservation all right?"

"Yes," he says, "everything is fine. I'm leaving at seven-thirty. They took me for a Frenchman, what a great feeling. I think it's because I'm wearing my black shirt. Well, maybe it's because it's a little dirty . . ."

"It's your haircut."

"You're right. Listen, thanks for everything. I miss it down there already. I'll write a long letter."

"Fine."

The evening is calm and clear. I am having dinner at the Jobs'. I leave the house about seven. There's plenty of time. The streets seem strangely quiet, perhaps I am no longer listening. Place du Carrouge. I cross the far side, glancing up. Her shutters are closed. I cannot tell if she is there. She will go home on the weekends now, I know, walking from the station in the dusk, the bicycles weaving past her, the voices soft. She shifts the suitcase from one hand to the other, her walk is a little uneven because of it, almost clumsy. She's wearing high heels. It takes her almost half an hour, the last part along the bank. The water in the canal lies flat. The light is going. Swallows are cutting across the fields in the dark. Madame Job, her face like an elbow, meets me at the door.

Before he boarded, the sun was already low at Orly. Almost no wind. A vast, malicious calm. In the distance, blue as winter, the dim roofs of the city. Smoke. The east growing dark. Aboard the plane all is brilliance. Dean sits at the window as they move, in the stillness of evening, towards the runway, the great tires bumping over the concrete joints. The seat-belt signs are lighted. The NO SMOKING is on. All of a sudden my imagination begins to panic, to rush from one thing to another. I have followed him so long I am sensitive to dangers. They turn smoothly into the direction for takeoff. All the perfect machinery of flight is beginning its motion. The huge, graceful wings are quivering. The engines roar. And now, at the last moment, it begins to move, slowly, with a majesty I cannot bear, for a long time seeming to go no faster until suddenly it is racing past, raising, clearing the ground. It climbs steeply. The soft darkness of the summer sky receives it. The lights grow fainter, the sound, and finally all of France, invisible now, silent, the France of all seasons deep in the silence of night, is left behind.

36

We meet in the Café Foy. It's like an empty railroad car with its bleak line of booths, its tables in the rear. The light of late afternoon fills it, the provincial calm. The *patron* is playing dominoes with a friend.

All alone, the day behind her, she walks back to where I am sitting and mechanically extends her hand. A single, downward shake which we are embarrassed by.

"*Bonjour,*" she says quietly.

"*Bonjour.*"

She sits with her eyes lowered, the bare table between us. It seems that the day is very white at the doorway, the white of clouded water. The traffic moves by without noise.

Dean was killed in a motor accident on the twelfth of June. There are only a few details. It was raining. It was at night. He was on his way to the country to visit his sister. Splinters of glass strewn everywhere, the rain thudding down. In each direction, waiting to pass, the line of cars, their headlights crowded, long lines, slow-moving like part of a great cortege. I could not believe the news. It seemed impossible, it seemed false, even if I'd expected it all along.

I feel I am looking at her endlessly before we speak—I am able to do it without her even noticing—and I see, as if nothing more had ever happened, the same girl who sat across the table at the Etoile d'Or, because suddenly she *is* the same, pale, uncertain, somehow resigned. It's exactly as if we are meeting for the first time. I can't think of what to say. It's hopeless. I simply don't know. Across from me is an ordinary girl, good-looking, not too intelligent perhaps. The silence begins to consume us. We sit in the narrow, empty room. I am facing the window, she the rear. I take her hand. As soon as I touch it, her eyes fill. She begins to cry. I look down. She knew it, she says. When she speaks the tears run down her face. She lets them. We sit without talking.

"Anne-Marie," I say, "what will you do? Will you stay in town here?"

She shrugs.

"I don't know," she murmurs.

"Perhaps it would be better if you went home."

"No," she says.

"I see. Are you sure?"

She nods.

"Well . . . you know, I'm going to be leaving, myself. I thought you might not want to stay here, and if you needed help going somewhere else, well, I'd be very happy to . . . do whatever I can. I mean, if you needed money . . ."

She seems not to be listening. *Merci,* she says.

It's very difficult. After a while I try to begin again. I ask about having dinner. She appears to consider it and finally shakes her head, no. I wait for her to talk about him, about herself, anything, but it never comes. The tears have stained her cheeks. She doesn't wipe them away. And it's here, in the Foy, that we say goodbye and then walk together to the door. Outside, the street is filled with shoppers. The cars are barely able to pass through. I

watch her cross; she moves by people, not touching them,
walking rather fast.

Perhaps—she is capable of this, I know—she will appear in the evening after all, down at the *gare,* coming
along the wide street alone, descending, as if merely on a
stroll. For in Dean's life, if there were such a thing, she
would come wherever he asked, no matter how far. She
would not hesitate. She would arrive to meet him, I know
exactly what she would do, how generous she would be,
how natural. And how sweet their first exchanges in the
language that she taught him.

37

M any fragments come to me, are discovered, reap-
pear. I wander about the room picking up or remembering things which are narcotic, which
induce me to dream—the details, the relics of love, suf-
fused with an aching beauty. In the back of a drawer I
find the lost portion of the list they made in Nancy, names
of hotels. It fits the other piece exactly. On it, the curious,
dead words: *Obelisk. Suez. Tous les Oiseaux du Monde.*
There is just one in her writing: *Ritz.*

The sunlight of that icy morning falls on my face
through enormous windows, through flats of glass with
tiny flaws, purified by bitter, Sunday silence. The smoke
floats blue in the cheap bars at dawn. The veterans cough.
Nancy, where she was born, where she learned to write in
that young, undistinguished hand:

> . . . there is nothing that is not yours, all I think, all
> I am able to feel. I am embarrassed only that I do
> not know enough. But I don't care if you never

belong to me, I only want to belong to you, just be hard with me, strict, but don't leave, just do like if you were with another girl—Please. I will die otherwise. I understand now that we can die of love.

I receive a letter from his father, sent on to me in Paris, asking me to forward the personal effects. Cristina will take care of that, she says. I assure her there isn't much. As for the car, it's a curious thing—it's registered in the name of Pritchard, 16 bis rue Jadin, and they know him. He's off in Greece for the summer, they think, but they'll handle that, too. Perhaps. It's parked under the trees near the house and locked, but like a very old man fading, it has already begun to crumble before one's eyes. The tires seem smooth. There are leaves fallen on the hood, the whitened roof. Around the wheels one can detect the first, faint discoloring of chrome. The leather inside, seen through windows which are themselves streaked blue, is dry and cracked. There it sits, this stilled machine, the electric clock on the dash ticking unheard, slowly draining the last of life. And one day the clock is wrong. The hands are frozen. It is ended.

Silence. A silence which comes over my life as well, I am not unwilling to express it. It is not the great squares of Europe that seem desolate to me, but the myriad small towns closed tight against the traveler, towns as still as the countryside itself. The shutters of the houses are all drawn. Only occasionally can one see the slimmest leak of light. The fields are becoming dark, the swallows shooting across them. I drive through these towns quickly. I am out of them before evening, before the neon of the cinemas comes on, before the lonely meals. I never spend the night.

But of course, in one sense, Dean never died—his existence is superior to such accidents. One must have heroes, which is to say, one must create them. And they become real through our envy, our devotion. It is we who give them their majesty, their power, which we ourselves could never possess. And in turn, they give some back. But they are mortal, these heroes, just as we are. They do not last forever. They fade. They vanish. They are surpassed, forgotten—one hears of them no more.

As for Anne-Marie, she lives in Troyes now, or did. She is married. I suppose there are children. They walk together on Sundays, the sunlight falling upon them. They visit friends, talk, go home in the evening, deep in the life we all agree is so greatly to be desired.

A NOTE ON THE TYPE

The principal text of this Modern Library edition
was composed in a digitized version of Palatino,
a contemporary typeface created by Hermann Zapf,
who was inspired by the sixteenth-century calligrapher
Giambattista Palatino, a writing master of Renaissance Italy.
Palatino was the first of Zapf's typefaces
to be introduced in America.